'It's too low,' said Bobby. 'It'll never make it over the hills.'

The Mystery Club could see what he meant. The aeroplane was coming to the far end of the loch. Unless the pilot pulled the nose up, there was the very real danger of it crashing into the hillside.

'Go on!' shouted Tracy. 'Higher! Go higher! Oh, for heaven's sake! What can we do?'

'Look!' shouted Holly. 'It's turning.'

'They must be looking for somewhere to land,' said Belinda.

The small plane rose as it turned back on itself, and then suddenly they could no longer hear the distant purr of the engine.

It was only a few seconds, but it felt like an eternity as the four of them watched the silent plane plunge into the trees on the far side of the loch.

A faint *whumph!* broke through the air and then there was only a deathly, horrifying silence.

The Mystery Club series

Crash Landing!
The Mystery Club 14

Fiona Kelly

Hodder
Children's
Books

a division of Hodder Headline plc

For John and Margaret MacCalman

Special thanks to Allan Frewin Jones for all his help

Copyright © by Ben M. Baglio
Created by Ben M. Baglio,
London W6 0HE

First published in Great Britain in 1995
by Hodder Children's Books

The right of Fiona Kelly to be identified as the Author of
the Work has been asserted by her in accordance with the
Copyright, Designs and Patents Act 1988.

10 9 8 7 6 5 4 3 2

A Catalogue record for this book is
available from the British Library

ISBN 0 340 63610 6

Typeset by Hewer Text Composition Services, Edinburgh
Printed and bound in Great Britain by
Cox & Wyman Ltd, Reading, Berkshire

Hodder Children's Books
a division of Hodder Headline plc
338 Euston Road
London NW1 3BH

1 Angel Bay

'I'm not at all sure about this,' said Mrs Adams as she sat on Holly's suitcase to get it closed. She grinned up at her daughter. 'Letting the three of you loose on Scotland without any supervision.'

Holly tucked her light brown hair behind her ears, her intelligent grey eyes shining. 'We'll be perfectly OK,' she said.

Mrs Adams laughed breathlessly as the case snapped shut. 'It wasn't you three I was worried about; it was everyone else in Scotland!'

'Anyone would think we were complete menaces!' said Holly. 'Besides,' she continued, picking up a book and shoving it into her shoulder-bag, 'we will be supervised, won't we? Christina McKetchnie will look after us.'

'I hope so,' said Mrs Adams. 'But according to Tracy's mum, Christina will have her hands full organising a charity concert up there.'

'There you are, then,' said Holly, picking another book off her shelf and cramming it into the already

1

overflowing shoulder-bag. 'We'll be kept out of mischief helping her.'

'Holly!' said Mrs Adams. 'Do you really need to take *all* your books with you? You're only going for a week, for heaven's sake.'

Reluctantly, Holly put the book back on the shelf. Her mystery novel shelf.

If there was one thing Holly loved, it was mysteries. Reading about them had been a passion of hers for years. But since she and her family had left London to live in Willow Dale, she had hardly had time to *read* about mysteries. She was too busy dealing with the real life mysteries that seemed to erupt all round her and her two companions in the Mystery Club.

The Adams family – Holly, her parents and her younger brother, Jamie – had come up to Yorkshire when Mrs Adams had been promoted to managership of her own branch of the bank she worked for. Mr Adams had cheerfully given up his job as a solicitor at the same time, to fulfill his lifelong ambition of earning a living by making beautiful wooden furniture. In a search for friends at her new school, Holly had come up with the idea of the Mystery Club. A special club dedicated to the pursuit of mysteries!

It was the three members of the Mystery Club who had been invited to stay at a guest-house in Scotland, at a place with the romantic name of Angel Bay, on the shores of Loch Evayne.

'Are you ready yet?' Mr Adams shouted up the stairs. 'We've got to pick up Tracy and Belinda and get you all to York in time for your train! How about getting a move on up there?'

'Coming,' called Mrs Adams.

It was not long before Holly's dad was honking the car horn outside the Fosters' house and Tracy Foster came charging down the path, her blonde hair bobbing and a huge smile on her face.

Next stop was at Belinda Hayes's house – a large chalet-style building at the posh end of the small Yorkshire town.

'Oh, Belinda!' sighed Tracy as Belinda crammed into the back seat with the others, her hair its usual bird's-nest tangle, and her eyes early-morning sleepy behind her wire-framed spectacles.

'What?' said Belinda.

'We're on holiday,' said Tracy. 'Couldn't you have worn something different?'

Belinda looked down at her baggy green sweatshirt and her faded jeans.

'I'm on holiday, right?' said Belinda.

'Yes,' agreed Tracy.

'So I can wear what I like, right?' said Belinda.

'I guess so,' sighed Tracy.

'Fine!' said Belinda, settling into the back seat of the Adams's Land-rover and pulling out a chocolate bar. 'End of conversation!'

Holly laughed. It was amazing how well her

two friends got on, considering how very different they were. Tracy was always full of energy and enthusiasm. Belinda said this was because she was half-American and didn't know any better. But then Belinda took everything at a much slower pace than most people. Her only real enthusiasm was for her thoroughbred horse. She had named it Meltdown, much to the horror of her society-hostess mother. Mrs Hayes often despaired of her daughter's casual approach to life – not that her mother's despair had any effect on Belinda.

It was quite a drive to the train station in York, and Mr Adams only just got them there in time.

'Have a good time,' he said as he helped them load their cases on to a trolley. 'I'm very jealous of you,' he said. 'I've always wanted to go to Scotland!'

The week long stay at Bay View Cottage had come out of the blue. Tracy's mother had been chatting on the phone to an old school friend of hers, Bruce McKetchnie, when he had mentioned that the guest-house run by his mother and father in Scotland was going to be empty for a week. A week that coincided with the three girls being off school.

It was too short notice for any of the girls' parents to take time off, and so it had been arranged that they would go up to Scotland on their own and be looked after by Bruce's mother, Christina McKetchnie.

A few phone calls and everything had been sorted out. Mrs McKetchnie was more than happy to have the girls stay, although, as Holly's mother pointed out in her usual dry way, that was because she didn't know what they were like.

She didn't know that Holly and the other two members of the Mystery Club attracted mysteries like magnets.

The train journey up to Scotland began, the three friends talking excitedly about what they wanted to do once they arrived.

The train carried them to Glasgow, where they had instructions to change on to another train that would take them on the final leg of their journey up to the little village of Glenroch.

The scenery was breathtaking. Holly had never been to Scotland before, and as the train wound its way up towards the western coast, she stared in awe at the great rearing crags that rose all round them. The mountains were *huge*. Towering up over them, tree-clad or boulder-strewn shoulders of rock, heaving up into the clear blue sky. Some of the loftier heights still had snow on them – like splashes of white paint from a giant's paint brush.

'We can go mountaineering,' Tracy said, her eyes shining as she stared out of the train window.

'*You* can, you mean,' Belinda replied, eyeing the formidable mountain peaks. 'You're not getting me up any mountains. They're taller than I am.'

Holly laughed. 'That's because they're older than you,' she said. 'Anyway, they're not called mountains. They're called Munros.' She waved a tourist brochure at them. 'It says so in here.'

Belinda settled lazily back in her seat. 'I'm not going Munro-eering, either,' she said. 'This is a holiday, not a survival course. Anyone got any food left?'

The train pulled into Glenroch station and the three girls hauled their cases out into the gravel parking area at the front of the station.

Glenroch was hardly even a village; it was just a small gathering of shops and houses on the road that led along the lower stretch of Loch Evayne towards the coast.

'Phew!' said Tracy, looking round at the sleepy, mountain-circled nest of grey and white buildings. 'Talk about remote!'

There was a car parked nearby, and even as the three girls dumped their cases on the gravel, the car door opened and a woman emerged.

'Aunt Christina!' called Tracy, running across to give the smiling woman a hug. 'It's so nice to see you again!'

'And you, my dear,' said Christina. 'It must be all of three years since we came down to visit. And

6

none of that *aunt* nonsense, if you don't mind. It makes me feel old!' She smiled. 'You're all to call me Christina.'

Tracy had explained to her two friends the background of how she knew the McKetchnies. Bruce McKetchnie had been a friend of Tracy's mother before she had ever met Tracy's American father and moved out to California. Tracy had been born out there, but the Fosters' marriage had failed and Mrs Foster had come back to her roots, only to find that Bruce was working in London, and that his parents had taken over the running of a guest-house in Scotland. Tracy had met the McKetchnies shortly after her return to Yorkshire three years earlier.

Holly and Belinda hovered in the background, smiling and waiting for Tracy to introduce them. Christina looked to be in her mid-fifties. She had neatly styled grey-blonde hair and a cheerful, young-looking face. She was wearing an attractive floral two-piece suit and wore muddy brogues on her feet.

All in all, thought Holly, she looked both friendly and capable. Just the sort of woman you could imagine running a busy guest-house. Holly liked her immediately.

Christina ushered them into the car and drove them along the narrow earthen road that led from the main highway and took them alongside the broad, silvery expanse of Loch Evayne.

7

'I'm afraid you're going to have to entertain yourselves for most of the time, although I shan't be far away if you need me,' she told them. 'My husband, John, is away up in Aberdeen for a couple of weeks, and I'm in the middle of organising a charity music concert in Glenroch. But there's plenty to do if you like the countryside.' She smiled round at them, her eyes sparkling. 'Although if you were hoping for any night life, I'm afraid you'll be disappointed. The nearest disco is seventy kilometres away.'

'That suits me,' Belinda said. 'Are there any horses?'

'No, I'm afraid not,' Christina said. 'But there are deer. And there's an old bull called Max who lives in a field nearby.'

'There you are,' Tracy said. 'How about having a go at bull-riding while you're up here, Belinda?'

'You catch it, and I'll ride it,' Belinda said.

Christina laughed. 'I can see you'll have no trouble keeping yourselves amused,' she said. 'Although I'd keep away from Max if I were you. He's a bad-tempered old fellow.'

Holly gazed round at her surroundings in delight. Thickets of reeds sprang up to one side of the narrow roadway, masking the long loch. To the other side was woodland and rugged meadows. As she looked round, the chimneys and high-sloping roof of a large building appeared through the trees.

'Is that where you live?' she asked.

8

'Good heavens, no,' Christina said. 'That's the Angel Hotel. Bay View is only a little cottage. But it's nearly three hundred years old, if that kind of thing interests you.'

If? Holly thought. *There are no 'ifs' about it!* The older a house was, in Holly's opinion, the more mysterious it was. And the more mysterious it was, the better Holly liked it.

A short drive took them over a small wooden bridge and into an open area of grass. Bay View Cottage lay, white and serene, behind a dry stone wall. It was a long, low stone building.

The three girls were met by a madcap golden retriever.

'This is Rosie,' Christina told them. 'As you'll find out, Rosie is in charge of everything. Rosie! Get down!' Christina looked apologetically at Holly as the friendly dog leaped up at her. 'She's a bit over-excited, I'm afraid. Rosie! I'm warning you!'

'It's OK,' said Holly with a laugh as Rosie nearly knocked her clean off her feet. 'I like dogs.'

Christina showed them up to their rooms. Holly and Belinda each had a small attractively decorated room with pine furniture and a single bed. Tracy had the third of the guest rooms – a larger room with a double bed.

The three girls unpacked quickly and wasted no time in coming back downstairs and phoning home to let their parents know they had arrived safely.

Afterwards, they walked down the stretch of grass that led to the shores of Loch Evayne. Beyond the grassy point, the loch curved to form a small bay with a sandy, seaweedy beach.

Mountains lifted grandly beyond the long expanse of the loch, their flanks green and grey and brown.

Tracy decided to have a game of fetch the stick with Rosie, but Holly and Belinda preferred to stretch themselves out on towels for a while and relax after their long trip.

Holly was lying on the beach, gazing happily up at the drifting streamers of thin summer cloud, when Christina's voice brought her out of her dream.

'Rosie! Good girl! Here girl!'

Holly smiled and stretched herself lazily in the sand. The sun shone fiercely above the mountains, sparkling on the rippled expanse of water beyond her feet.

Rosie raced past the towels.

Belinda spluttered and sat up as drops of water splashed over her.

'Someone's been encouraging Rosie to go into the water, I see,' said Christina as Tracy came running up. 'I forgot to tell you about the house rule. Anyone who lures Rosie into the loch has to give her a bath afterwards.'

'Oh, I'm sorry,' said Tracy. 'I didn't realise.'

Christina laughed. 'I was only joking with you,'

she said. 'Rosie doesn't need any encouragement to get herself wet. But I'd appreciate if you'd make sure she stays outside until she dries off a bit. I've made some sandwiches, if anyone's hungry.'

The three girls gathered their towels and followed Christina into the house.

'That's the dining-room,' said Christina, pointing into a room dominated by a long table. 'But I've put out the sandwiches in the sitting-room. And you'll find a few maps and local guides in there as well.'

The sitting-room, like all the other rooms in the cottage, was small and cosy and looked newly decorated.

Belinda plumped down in an armchair and attacked the sandwiches while Holly and Tracy looked through the various pamphlets and leaflets that Christina had put out for them.

Through the window they could see Rosie racing about in the garden, chasing butterflies.

Holly opened up a map. It showed the ragged west coast and a sea dotted with islands. Loch Evayne thrust inland like a long bent finger, about twenty kilometres long.

'Is the loch very deep?' she asked.

'In the middle it is,' said Christina. 'All the lochs are deep. That's why we have legends like the Loch Ness monster – because no one really knows what goes on in the depths. Loch Ness is nearly two hundred and thirty metres deep in some places.'

'I don't suppose you have a Loch Evayne monster, do you?' asked Tracy. 'I'd love to take some photos of a real monster. We could print them in the school magazine, couldn't we, Holly? New monster found in a Scottish loch.'

'If there is one, it's kept itself to itself,' said Christina. 'But we do have other legends, you know. Stories of strange creatures up in the mountains. And weird, ghostly things seen by lone walkers in the twilight.'

Holly's ears pricked up. 'What sort of *things*?' she asked.

Christina smiled. 'People have reported seeing a hairy creature up in the crags. It's never been photographed, but the stories say it's a werewolf.'

Belinda stopped chewing, her eyes round. 'A werewolf? Crumbs! Well, that fixes it. I'm keeping well away from those mountains.'

'You're such a coward,' said Tracy. She looked excitedly at Christina. 'What else?'

'There's the story of the lost boy,' said Christina. 'A young lad who died up on the mountains a long time ago. Sometimes he appears to people and offers them water from a leather bottle. And if they drink from the bottle, they're taken off to strange, wild places and are never seen again.'

'So, generally it's not a good idea to take water from anyone you meet up on the mountains, I suppose,' said Holly. 'Especially not from young boys.'

12

'Wait a minute,' said Belinda. 'If these people disappear and are never seen again, how does anyone *know* that they met the lost boy?'

'Because one man escaped to tell the tale,' said Christina with a dark smile.

'You're having us on,' Belinda said with a grin. 'I don't believe a word of it.'

'Everyone says that,' said Christina. 'Until they catch a glimpse of the werewolf, or encounter the lost boy. I'm not saying it's true. I'm just *warning* you. And I haven't told you yet of the Callach Vair – the Old Woman of the Hills.'

'What does she offer people?' asked Belinda. 'Ghostly cups of tea and phantom scones?'

Christina laughed. 'She doesn't offer anything,' she said. 'She was turned to stone in the old days. You can see her, standing alone on the hillside, as a constant warning to all who pass by.'

The three girls listened, spellbound, as Christina told them more legends of the remote crags round Loch Evayne. Of the ancient clansman who had been seen in the upper mists, barring the way forwards with a claymore in one hand and the severed head of an Englishman in the other. Of the ghastly Lord of Weir, whose eerie pipe-playing led unwary travellers to the phantom Castle of Weir high on Ben Cruachan. And of an entire family of cannibal ghosts who lived in a cavern away up in the mountains, and who dined off the flesh of lost walkers.

At the end, Christina laughed and clapped her hands, breaking the spell she had woven. 'So, you can't say you haven't been warned,' she said. 'Although, if you meet *any* of those people, it'll be more than I've ever done – and I've been living here for over fifteen years.'

'Let's organise a ghost-hunt!' said Holly. 'I want to visit all those places you mentioned. I could write a really brilliant report for the magazine next term.'

'It's a bit late to be wandering up on the mountains today,' said Christina. 'You wouldn't even get to the foothills before nightfall. And if you want to do any real exploring up there, you're going to need a guide. All those ghost stories I told you might not be true, but people do get lost up there – and I don't think you'd enjoy a night up on the mountains. When the mist comes down, you could get lost in minutes.' She smiled. 'But if you fancy a ramble before dinner, you could always take yourselves off through the woods. That should help you work up an appetite.'

'I don't really need to work up an appetite,' said Belinda. 'My appetite seems to work itself up without any help from me.'

'Don't be so lazy,' said Tracy, jumping up. 'Hands up everyone who wants to go for a walk.'

Holly and Tracy put their hands up.

'You're outvoted,' said Tracy, dragging Belinda out of her comfortable chair.

'OK, OK,' said Belinda. 'But I'm not going far. And if I see anything weird out there, I'm going to make sure it gets you first.'

'Don't worry,' said Christina. 'I've never heard tell of any strange goings on down here. All our local fiends seem to prefer the wilds of the mountaintops. You've got an hour before dinner will be ready.'

'I'll act as guide,' said Tracy. 'I'm brilliant at orienteering.'

'Since when?' said Belinda.

'I've always been great at finding my way around,' said Tracy, as the three of them stepped out through the front door and were met by a cool breeze off the loch.

'Smell that air!' said Holly, taking a deep breath. 'Isn't it wonderful? Which way shall we go?'

Belinda crossed her eyes and pointed in two different directions. 'That way,' she said.

'This way,' said Tracy, heading away from the path and towards some trees.

'Remember,' called Christina, 'dinner is in one hour.'

Tracy led her two friends into the trees.

Holly looked at her watch. 'If we walk in this direction for half an hour,' she said, 'then turn round and retrace our steps, we'll be back just in time for dinner.'

They walked together for a while in the cool,

dark shade of the trees, chatting about their plans for the week.

Tracy came to a sudden halt and Belinda almost bumped into her back.

'Tracy!' exclaimed Belinda, readjusting her spectacles. 'Don't do that.'

'Shh! Look!' whispered Tracy.

'What is it?' said Belinda, peering over her friend's shoulder. 'A werewolf?'

'No. Rabbits,' said Tracy.

The three girls became quite still. A little way off they could see three or four little brown shapes scampering through the undergrowth.

'There must be a warren nearby,' whispered Holly. 'Don't move or you'll startle them.'

But it was already too late. The rabbits lifted their small, blunt heads and seemed to be listening, their noses twitching. A second later, there was the flash of white cotton-wool tails as the rabbits hopped away out of sight.

Tracy put her finger to her lips and crept after them.

'Shouldn't we be getting back?' said Belinda, ten minutes later. There had been no further sight of the rabbits.

'Tracy,' said Holly, 'she's right. We've been gone over half an hour. Let's go back.'

'Oh, OK,' sighed Tracy. 'Maybe we'll find the warren another day.'

They retraced their steps.

Holly looked anxiously at her watch. 'Are you sure you're leading us the right way?' she asked Tracy a few minutes later.

'Sure I am,' said Tracy, her American accent suddenly becoming a lot more obvious, as it always did when she was excited or worried.

Belinda came to a halt, her hands on her hips.

'We're lost, aren't we?' she said. 'I knew this was going to happen if we trusted Tracy.'

'We're not *lost*,' said Tracy. 'I'm just not sure where we are.'

Belinda stared at her. 'What's the difference?'

'There's a big difference between being totally lost and *temporarily* not knowing which way to go,' said Tracy.

'We should head for the loch,' said Holly. 'It's easy.'

'And which way is that?' asked Belinda.

'Um,' Holly peered through the trees. 'That way?'

'No, *that* way,' insisted Tracy, pointing in another direction.

'Brilliant!' said Belinda. 'Absolutely brilliant!'

'What was that noise?' said Holly.

They all heard it. A furtive rustling sound as if someone – or something – was moving stealthily through the bushes nearby. The hair stood up on Holly's neck as Christina's creepy stories came back to her.

17

The three girls moved closer together, all uncomfortably aware that the atmosphere of the woodland had changed. It was as if the woods had become watchful.

'I wouldn't mind getting out of here,' murmured Belinda.

'It was probably just an animal,' said Tracy. 'A deer or something. Can you see anything?'

'No,' said Holly, straining her eyes into the tangle of bushes and trees that hemmed them in.

There was another rustle – from closer by this time, and Holly thought she saw a movement out of the corner of her eye.

'We know you're there,' called Tracy. 'Come on out. You're not scaring us, you know.'

There was a low growl. The three girls nearly jumped out of their skins as a tall clump of bushes began to rattle and sway.

With a stifled yell, Belinda turned and ran.

Holly and Tracy stared at each other for a split second before taking to their heels.

And as they ran, crashing and blundering through the dense woodland, Holly was certain that she heard the sound of pursuing feet.

2 Lost and found

Their headlong flight didn't last long. Belinda's foot caught on a hidden root and she fell, sprawling on the ground, bringing Tracy down on top of her with a breathless shriek.

Holly leaned against a tree trunk, panting as she stared back the way they had come.

The woods were eerily silent. No half-imagined shape came charging out of the bushes at them. And there was no sound other than that of their own loud breathing and a groan from Belinda as she untangled herself from Tracy's legs and sat up.

'Why did you run like that?' gasped Holly.

'I don't know,' said Belinda. 'I thought there was something there. Why did *you* run?'

'I thought you'd seen something,' said Tracy as she picked herself up. '*Was* there anything?'

'I thought I heard something,' said Holly. 'But whatever it was, it's gone now.' She grinned at her friends, suddenly feeling a little foolish. 'It was probably a deer. Didn't Mrs McKetchnie say there were deer round here?'

19

'Deer don't growl,' said Belinda.

'You heard that, too, did you?' said Holly. 'I thought maybe I'd imagined it.'

'It could have been a wolf,' said Tracy.

'Don't be daft,' said Belinda. 'There aren't any wolves in Scotland.' She clambered to her feet, brushing the debris from the woodland floor off her sweat-shirt. 'Can we please try and find our way out of this place?'

'What we really need is a compass,' said Tracy. 'I could get us back to the cottage in no time if I had a compass.'

Belinda sighed. 'We haven't got a compass, Tracy.'

'I know how to make one,' said Tracy. 'All you need is a bowl of water, a cork and a magnetised needle. You push the needle through the cork and put it in the water. The needle will always point north.' She grinned. 'You see? I'm not as useless as you think.'

'OK,' said Belinda. 'You get the magnetised needle out, Tracy. Holly? Do you want to look for a bowl of water while I root around for a cork? We'll be out of here in two shakes of a werewolf's tail!'

Tracy frowned at Belinda. 'At least I'm trying to be constructive,' she said. 'Why don't you come up with an idea, if you think mine are so dumb?'

'OK, I will,' said Belinda. She looked up into

the spreading branches above their heads. 'Now, where's the sun?'

'Of course,' said Holly. 'That's it! The sun is over on the far side of the loch. So all we have to do is walk towards the sun until we hit the water. Well done, Belinda.'

'That was my next plan,' said Tracy.

The three girls cast about for some telltale glimpse of brightness through the dense canopy of leaves. The sun had to be *somewhere* up there – it was just a case of locating it and heading in that direction.

'If you ask me,' said Tracy, 'it's gone down behind the mountains.' Her eyes suddenly lit up. 'The mountains!' she said. 'The nearest mountains are on the other side of the loch. We head towards them!'

'I can't see any mountains either,' said Holly. 'There are too many trees around.'

'Let's find the tallest tree,' said Tracy. 'I'll climb up it. I'll be able to see better from up in the air.'

'At last,' said Belinda. 'Tracy's had a good idea. At least that makes up for you getting us into this mess in the first place.'

It didn't take them long to find a tall tree that looked like it could be climbed. Low branches spread out like spokes just above Tracy's head.

'You'll be careful, won't you?' said Holly as Tracy circled the tree, looking for a sturdy branch. 'We don't want you falling out and breaking your leg.'

21

'I won't fall,' Tracy said confidently. She grinned. 'And if I do, I'll make sure I fall on Belinda. She'll make for a nice soft landing.'

'Oi!' exclaimed Belinda. 'What's that supposed to mean? Are you suggesting I'm fat?'

'No. Just soft,' said Tracy. 'Now! Stand by for blast-off.' She crouched, her eyes fixed on the chosen branch, her muscles tensing for the spring.

She jumped, stretching her arms up and catching hold of the branch. Tracy swung there for a second, her feet dangling, and then slowly pulled herself up.

'Go for it, Tracy!' called Belinda. 'You can do it!'

Tracy got an elbow over the branch and swung a leg up.

'Do you need any help?' asked Holly.

'No,' panted Tracy. 'I'm doing fine.' She hooked her foot over the branch.

'Hey! Get down from there!' The sudden voice made Holly jump. A boy's voice shouting from behind her. She hardly had time to look round before a figure burst out of cover and almost knocked her over as it rushed towards the tree.

'What the heck!' gasped Tracy. It was a teenage boy, dressed in jeans and a green jacket, his hair a flare of red as he ran at the tree and caught hold of Tracy's dangling leg.

'Get off me, you idiot!' Tracy shouted as the boy yanked at her foot.

It only took Holly a second to recover from her shock, and she and Belinda leaped at the boy, grabbing at his jacket and trying to pull him away. But it was too late. Tracy lost her grip on the branch and fell, crashing down on to the boy and sending all four of them sprawling on the ground.

'Oh!' gasped the boy, floundering under Tracy's weight. He clearly hadn't expected to find himself flattened into the ground.

Tracy sat up, glaring angrily at him. 'What do you think you're doing?' she yelled. 'Are you crazy, or something?'

The boy sat up. 'You can't climb that tree,' he gasped. 'I had to stop you.'

'Who do you think you are?' yelled Tracy. 'I could have been hurt, you great dumb jerk!'

The boy blinked at her. 'You're American,' he said. 'I thought you were all English from your voices earlier.'

'What the heck has that got to do with anything?' said Tracy.

Holly picked herself up. 'And what do you mean by *earlier*?' she said. 'Have you been following us?'

The boy grinned at them. 'You didn't take much following,' he said. 'I could have tracked you blindfolded, the noise you were making.' He stood up, straightening his jacket. 'I've been on your trail for the last half hour.' He smiled at Tracy. 'I liked the idea about the floating compass.'

Tracy stared at him. 'You . . . you . . . ' She seemed at a loss for words.

Holly looked closely at the boy. He seemed to be about their age, or maybe a little younger, with a face full of freckles, a broad, toothy grin and a wild thatch of bright red hair. His blue eyes were full of humour as he stood grinning at them.

'Look,' said the boy, 'I'm sorry about pulling you down out of that tree. But I couldn't let you disturb the ospreys. Their nest is up there. If you had frightened them off they might have abandoned their chicks. Ospreys are very timid birds. I couldn't risk it. I didn't hurt you, did I?'

'Ospreys?' said Holly, gazing up into the tree. 'They're really rare, aren't they?'

'*Very* rare,' said the boy. 'There are only about half a dozen mating couples in the entire area. That's why I was trying to keep you away.'

'Oh, I get it,' said Belinda. 'The growling and the rustling in the bushes. That was you, was it?'

The boy grinned apologetically. 'I was just trying to scare you off,' he said. 'I didn't mean you to get lost.'

'Why didn't you just tell us?' said Holly. 'Why all the creeping about?'

The boy scratched his head. 'It's better if people don't know where the ospreys are,' he said. 'People

24

come from all over to look at them. They even steal the eggs. And then the ospreys abandon their nest. I didn't want to risk that happening.'

'We wouldn't have done anything to harm them,' said Belinda. 'What sort of people do you think we are?'

'Yeah, OK, I take your point,' said the boy. 'But it's better to be safe than sorry. And you must promise me you won't tell anyone else where the nest is.'

'Of course we won't,' said Holly.

'Why don't you put warning signs up?' said Belinda.

The boy laughed. 'What? This way to the secret osprey nest? Please keep away! I don't think so. Are you up here on holiday?'

'We're staying at Bay View Cottage,' said Tracy.

'With Mrs McKetchnie?' said the boy. 'That's nice for you.'

Tracy looked at him. 'Are you some kind of forest ranger, then?' she asked. '*Junior* division?'

'No,' said the boy. 'I wish I was. I've got a holiday job at the Angel Hotel. My parents live away down in Inverary so I've got a wee room in the hotel. I work mostly in the kitchens, but I keep an eye on the ospreys as often as I can. My name's Bobby Talisker.'

'I'm Tracy Foster,' said Tracy. 'And this is Holly Adams and Belinda Hayes.'

'Now we've all been introduced,' said Belinda, 'do you think you could show us the way out of here?'

'With pleasure,' said Bobby. 'Follow me.'

He led them confidently through the trees and it wasn't long before they came out of the woodland and saw, across a bank of tall reeds, the long silver waters of Loch Evayne with the mountains lifting beyond.

'We're about half a kilometre north of the cottage,' Bobby told them as they walked alongside the reedbed. 'I'll come with you. I've got to get back to the hotel anyway. Where are you from?'

'Yorkshire,' said Belinda. 'Although Tracy's from California originally, and Holly's a newcomer from London.'

'So how did you meet up?' asked Bobby.

'We go to the same school,' said Holly. 'We're a kind of club.'

'What? Just the three of you?' asked Bobby. 'What sort of club is it?'

'We call ourselves the Mystery Club,' said Holly. 'Do you like mystery novels? Have you ever heard of P. J. Benson? She's my favourite author.'

Bobby shook his head. 'I don't read much,' he said. 'So what does your club do? Anything interesting?'

The three girls looked at one another. Now

26

that was a question that would take a *lot* of answering.

'It works like this,' said Belinda. 'Holly gets us into trouble, Tracy makes it worse, and then I have to get us out of it. For instance, there was this time when Tracy managed to get herself kidnapped, and— '

'Kidnapped?' interrupted Bobby. 'You're having me on!'

'Don't you believe it,' said Belinda. 'I'm telling you, the weirdest things happen when Holly's around. Even when we're on holiday, she's always looking for some kind of hair-raising adventure. She's just not safe to be with.' She looked at Holly and Tracy. 'Right now, this pair want us to go hunting for werewolves in the mountains, would you believe.'

Bobby laughed. 'You've heard some of the local legends, then, have you? And what would you do if you found a werewolf?'

'Interview it,' said Holly with a laugh. 'For our school magazine.' She lifted her hand in the pretence of holding a microphone. 'Mr Werewolf,' she said, 'would you like to tell our readers a little about yourself?'

Belinda made a growling noise. 'It's not so bad being a werewolf,' she said huskily. 'I only have to go on the prowl when there's a full moon. And I'm covered in all this shaggy fur, so I don't get too cold. Hmm, I'm feeling a bit peckish. Do you mind if I sink my fangs into your neck for a few minutes, Holly?'

'You're crackers,' said Bobby.

'Yeah,' said Tracy. 'I've been telling them that for months. I'm the only sane one in – hey! Look, guys! An aeroplane.' She had caught sight of it out of the corner of her eye – a small dark sliver, outlined against the mountains as it moved over the loch.

They all looked. At that distance it looked like a toy. A small aeroplane, skimming low over the water, the sound of its engine coming to them as a faint, shuddering purr.

'That doesn't sound right,' said Bobby. 'The engine shouldn't be making noises like that.' They could all hear it now. The purr would rise to a growling cough and then fade before breaking into another scratchy roar. And the aeroplane wasn't flying straight, either. It rose and dipped as if the pilot was having difficulty controlling it.

'It's in trouble,' gasped Holly. 'Oh, no! it's going to crash!'

The aeroplane lurched, and for a few terrible moments it really did look as though it was going to plunge into the loch. But then the nose lifted and it continued on its erratic way across the dark backdrop of the mountains.

'It's too low,' said Bobby. 'It'll never make it over the hills.'

They could see what he meant. The aeroplane was coming to the far end of the loch. Unless the pilot managed to gain control and pull the nose up, there was the very real danger of the aeroplane crashing into the tree-clad hillside.

'Go on!' shouted Tracy. 'Higher! Go higher!' Oh, for heaven's sake! What can we do?'

'Look!' shouted Holly. 'It's turning.' The slender cigar shape of the aeroplane changed to a cross as it banked and cut a tight curve across the loch.

'They must be looking for somewhere to land,' said Belinda.

The small plane rose as it turned back on itself, and then suddenly they could no longer hear the distant purr of the engine.

It was only a few seconds, but it felt like an eternity as the four of them watched the silent plane lose height and plunge into the trees on the far side of the loch.

A faint *whumph!* broke through the air and then there was only a deathly, horrifying silence.

3 The crash site

'We've got to get help,' cried Holly, tearing her eyes away from the scene of the crash, her face as white as chalk. There was no sign of the crashed aeroplane. It was as if the trees had simply swallowed it up.

'We can phone from the cottage,' said Tracy. She ran, her feet pounding on the rugged grass as she sprinted ahead of the others. Bobby was after her in a moment, Holly and Belinda only a few paces behind him.

Tracy was soon several metres ahead of the others as she ran sure-footedly along the narrow path. Her arms pumped at her sides, her eyes fixed determinedly on the distance as she brought all her strength into play. She knew she was faster than Holly and Belinda, but five hundred metres was a long way to run at full speed, and she couldn't afford to make any mistakes over the bumpy, uneven terrain.

She knew how remote this area was. The chances were that she and her friends were the only people

31

to have seen the crash. The pilot's life might depend on them getting help as quickly as possible. Unless, of course, the pilot was already . . . *No!* Tracy refused to think about that as she redoubled her efforts and left the other three trailing in her wake.

At last! She saw the first glimpse of the white cottage in the distance. She ran as she had never run before, gathering herself to vault the low stone wall. Rosie the dog came racing round the side of the cottage, barking and thrashing her tail. She jumped up at Tracy so she was almost knocked off her feet.

Tracy dodged round the frisking dog and threw herself through the door.

'Christina!' she yelled. 'There's been a crash! We have to get help!'

Christina came running out from the dining-room, wearing a pinafore and wiping her hands on a towel.

'Good Lord! Where?' she asked. 'What sort of crash?'

'An aeroplane!' panted Tracy. 'Over on the far side of the loch. We saw it come down.'

'I'll phone,' said Christina. 'Stay by me. You can tell them exactly where it came down.'

Christina punched out a number on the phone. Tracy stood by her side, doubled over with her hands on her knees as she fought for breath.

*   *   *

Belinda was way behind the others, running as fast as she could but plagued by a stitch that gnawed into her side. Ahead of her, Holly and Bobby were running almost neck and neck as they approached the cottage.

By the time Belinda scrambled over the stone wall, the others were all in the cottage and Tracy was speaking rapidly into the telephone.

'I think I know where you mean,' said Christina as Tracy tried to pinpoint the place where the aeroplane had gone down. 'Tell them it's near Iron Stone Croft. They'll know it.'

Tracy breathlessly relayed this information down the phone. She put the receiver down and collapsed on to the arm of the sofa, her hand to her aching chest.

'They're on their way!' she panted.

'It's a thirty kilometre drive from the fire station,' gasped Bobby. 'They've got to go right round the end of the loch.' He stared at Christina. 'And it's just a dirt track. It could take them half an hour.'

'Isn't there anything we could do?' asked Holly.

'Yes!' exclaimed Christina. 'We could get across the loch in half that time. Bobby, come with me – we'll use the boat. Holly – there's a first-aid box in the boot of my car. The car keys are hanging by the door.' She pulled off her pinafore as she ran to the door. 'Belinda – run through to the kitchen

for me and turn everything off, will you, please?'
She looked at Tracy. 'I think you should stay here,
dear. You've done enough already.'

'No way!' said Tracy. 'I'm coming with you. I've
done a first-aid course at school.'

'Quickly, then,' said Christina.

Holly snatched down the keys from the hook by
the door and ran to the car as the others raced down
to the loch.

Holly had seen the boat earlier; a small motor-
cruiser moored at the side of a long wooden jetty
some two hundred metres along the bank of the
loch. Christina had promised them a ride in it
at some stage but Holly had never expected the
ride to come so quickly – or in such terrible
circumstances.

She pulled the red first-aid box out of the boot
of the car and chased after the others. Christina,
Bobby and Tracy were already in the boat and
Belinda was untying the mooring hawser as Holly's feet thudded along the wooden boards of
the jetty.

The roar of the motor sounded as Holly and
Belinda jumped aboard. Christina swung the wheel
and the boat glided away from the jetty, quickly
picking up speed as it sliced through the water.
The seaweed-encrusted shore of the loch dropped
behind them as Christina stood at the wheel and
sent the small boat shooting out across the loch.

White water churned behind them and as Holly glanced back she saw Rosie at the end of the jetty, barking madly.

Tracy stood at the cabin door, her knuckles white as she gripped the rail and stared ahead, her eyes searching for any sign of where the aeroplane had come down.

'There!' she shouted, pointing. A trail of grey smoke drifted out of the trees. 'Over there! Can't we go any faster?'

'We're at full speed now,' said Christina.

'Is it on fire?' asked Belinda. 'I can't see any flames.'

Holly tried not to think about what they might find. But at least it hadn't looked as though the aeroplane had plummetted nose first into the trees. Maybe the pilot had managed to find a gap in the trees wide enough for a safe landing. But as Holly stared out across the loch, the thin ribbons of smoke that lifted into the air brought her heart up into her throat. Could anyone survive such a crash?

Away to their left, a solitary hump-backed island rose out of the loch. Christina had told them its name: Innis Maer. A dark, brooding lump of rock, scattered with greenery and girdled with seaweed.

The forested rim of the loch was approaching rapidly now. But apart from the telltale smoke, there was still no sign of the aeroplane.

'I daren't go too close,' said Christina, as she turned the wheel and brought the boat round. 'There may be rocks under the surface. Bobby, throw the anchor over when I give the word. I'll get in as close as I can.'

Holly could see the concentration in her face as she slowed the boat and steered it nearer and nearer to the shoreline. Beyond the lapping water was a deep line of seaweed, then a metre or two of gravelly sand before the trees began their dense march up the hillside.

'Now!' cried Christina. There was a splash as Bobby let the anchor drop from the back of the boat and Christina cut the engine.

Tracy was over the side first, clinging on for a moment as she let her legs down into the cold water. She let go and the water rose round her waist as her feet hit the bottom.

'It's OK,' she shouted up. 'It's not too deep.'

The bed of the loch rose steeply, and in five paces Tracy was out of the water and running over the seaweed.

The others followed her, Holly catching her breath as the cold water enveloped her legs. She turned in the waist-deep water to help Belinda.

A fountain of chilly water splashed over her as Bobby plunged over the side, the first-aid box under his arm.

There was no time to think about the cold

as they waded up to the shore and ran after Tracy.

Now they could see the path the aeroplane had cut through the trees. There were smashed and broken branches. A white section of wing lay against a tree trunk and the earth was churned up and scattered with pieces of metal.

The aeroplane had come to rest between two trunks, its tail in the air and its nose buried in a tangle of snapped branches and heaved-up earth. The small door was hanging open, and beyond the door, Holly could see the source of the smoke. The engine was on fire. Bright, greedy flames licked up round the aeroplane's front, catching the nearby branches and leaves with a dry, crackling sound.

'Keep back!' shouted Bobby. 'It's not safe!'

But Tracy was already at the side of the aeroplane, stamping at the spreading flames. Holly wrenched her jacket off and ran forwards, beating at the fire, the intense heat scalding her skin.

The others joined her, flailing at the fire with branches, gradually beating it back and stamping at the smouldering undergrowth.

Out of the corner of her eye, Holly saw Tracy reach through the open door of the cockpit. She pulled out a red canister and a few seconds later there was a fierce hissing as she set off the fire extinguisher. A blanket of foam finally snuffed the flames out round the nose of the aeroplane.

'Where's the pilot?' gasped Belinda, wiping her hand across her sweating forehead. The little one-person cockpit was empty. A branch had smashed the windscreen, scattering shards of glass over the seat.

'He must have pulled himself free,' said Holly.

'Unless he was thrown out,' said Bobby, running to the back of the aeroplane and forcing his way through the hanging branches. 'I can't see anyone.'

'He must be nearby,' said Christina. 'Spread out. We've got to find him.'

Holly noticed an ominous smear of blood on the windscreen where the broken glass still hung in its frame. The pilot's head must have hit the glass.

They scattered, searching all round the aeroplane.

Belinda bit her lip – half-hoping and half-dreading to find the pilot. But there was no sign of anyone. What had happened? Had he been flung from the aeroplane as it crashed? Or had he staggered away for fear of the fire spreading? Was he lying semi-conscious, hidden by undergrowth?

The five of them gathered again by the aeroplane. No one had found any sign of the pilot. It was as if he had vanished into the air.

Christina ran her fingers through her hair. 'If he banged his head, he could have concussion,' she said. 'Or maybe he was able to go for help.' She looked at her watch. 'The rescue people should be here soon.'

'What do we do?' asked Tracy, shivering from cold and exertion. 'Do we just wait?'

Christina put her arm round Tracy's shoulders. 'You must be frozen,' she said. Tracy nodded, her teeth chattering. 'There's no point in us all staying here,' said Christina. 'There's nothing else we can do now.'

'You go back,' said Bobby. 'I'll hang on here until the rescue people arrive.'

'Are you sure?' said Holly. 'Surely we can search some more.' She couldn't help imagining the pilot lying bleeding and helpless amongst the trees. The thought of giving up and leaving him was dreadful.

'Bobby's right,' said Christina. 'If he was nearby, we'd have found him. The chances are that he's wandered off somewhere in search of help.' She gave Holly a reassuring smile. 'They'll find him,' she said. 'Don't you worry. Bobby, will you be OK on your own? I think I ought to get the girls back home.'

'I'll be fine,' said Bobby. 'I'll stay by the plane until they get here. I'll let them know what happened.'

It wasn't until Holly came out from under the canopy of the trees that she noticed how dark it had got. Away to the east the sky was a deep blue,

39

and at her back the mountains rose up black against the fading light.

Christina waded out to the gently bobbing boat and pulled herself on board, leaning over to help the girls up one by one out of the chilling water.

'There are a couple of blankets in the cabin,' she said as she hauled up the anchor. 'Wrap yourselves up in them.'

Holly found the blankets and the three girls huddled together in the back of the boat, their arms round one another as the boat headed off back across the darkening water.

'I hope they find the pilot before it gets dark,' said Tracy, shivering between her two friends. 'It would be terrible if he was just left to wander round there at night.'

'Of course they'll find him,' Holly said as brightly as she could.

Belinda looked anxiously at Tracy's pale face. 'You ought to get a medal – the way you tackled that fire,' she said. She looked across at Holly. 'Did you see her? Fearless Foster the demon fire-fighter! And the way you ran! I bet you broke some records there.'

Tracy smiled wanly. 'I guess I did,' she said. 'Sorry, guys – I'm *so* cold.'

Christina McKetchnie glanced round. 'It's the shock,' she said. 'Don't worry. You'll be home soon.'

The boat came to a bumping halt against the jetty. As they headed towards the cottage, Holly looked over her shoulder. The far side of the loch was shrouded in darkness now and the sky was beginning to sparkle with stars.

Rosie was waiting for them by the door. She nuzzled Tracy's hand, her big brown eyes looking up at her as if she knew something bad had happened.

'OK,' said Christina. 'I want the three of you out of those wet things and into the shower as quick as you can. I'll get dinner going again. We could all do with something warm inside us.'

Holly went into her room and peeled off her soaking clothes. She wrapped herself in her dressing-gown and went to see how Belinda was doing.

Belinda was at her window, peering out into the night.

'Can you see those lights?' she said to Holly. Away in the distance, the pinpoints of flickering blue lights could just be made out in the blackness. 'That must be the rescue vehicle, don't you think?'

'I hope so,' said Holly. 'And I really hope they've found that poor pilot. What do you think can have happened?'

'Maybe he ran out of fuel,' said Belinda. 'Or maybe the engine just conked out on him. Is Tracy OK?'

'I think so,' said Holly. 'I heard her go into the bathroom.'

'She was brilliant, wasn't she?' said Belinda.

Holly smiled. 'I'll tell her you said that,' she said.

'No, don't do that,' said Belinda with a grin. 'I've already dished out one lot of praise for her. If I do it again, she'll start expecting it, and we'll never hear the end of it. Do you want to toss a coin for the next in the shower – or shall we do it alphabetically?'

'I don't mind,' said Holly, her eyes fixed on that glittering point of blue light in the far distance as she quietly prayed that the missing pilot would be found alive and well.

Their holiday had certainly started dramatically. She only hoped that the morning would bring good news.

4 Manhunt

Holly awoke early the next morning. She was out of bed in an instant, the details of last night's aeroplane crash flooding back into her mind as she pulled her clothes on. She drew the curtains back.

It was a beautiful scene. The sky was clear and blue above the ridges of the greeny-brown mountains. The waters of the loch sparkled. Even the humped island – Innis Maer – seemed less gloomy in daylight, lifting itself out in the middle of the long loch like the back of a whale.

It was difficult to believe that those dark green trees away in the distance held such a dreadful secret.

Belinda's room was next to Holly's. She knocked on Belinda's door.

'Are you up yet?' she called.

'Yes,' came a drowsy voice from beyond the pine door.

Holly pushed the door open. Belinda was in bed – much as Holly had suspected. Holly heard a door open further along the hallway.

It was Tracy, up and dressed and looking fully recovered from their adventures.

'Do you think Christina will have heard anything yet?' Holly asked Tracy as she came along to Belinda's room. 'Belinda, what are you doing in bed still?'

'Being woken up,' said Belinda, reaching for her spectacles. 'As *usual*. Give me five minutes, can't you?'

But her two friends had no intention of leaving her to get up in her own time. They pulled the bedcovers off Belinda and dragged her out ignoring all protests.

A few minutes later the three of them were down in the dining-room. The long table was set for breakfast. Music drifted out of the kitchen.

'Good morning,' said Christina, smiling as she came out of the kitchen. 'Did you all sleep well?'

'Like a log,' said Tracy.

'Has there been any news?' asked Holly.

'I've just put the radio on,' said Christina. 'There'll be a local news bulletin in five minutes. There should be something on that. If you'd like to take a seat, I'll bring some toast through. I'm making a proper cooked breakfast for you.'

'Are we getting porridge?' asked Belinda.

'You can have some porridge if you'd like some,' said Christina.

'Not really,' said Belinda. 'I don't much like it, to

be honest. I just thought, you know, with us being in Scotland – we might be expected to eat it.'

Christina laughed. 'We don't all live on porridge up here,' she said.

Belinda blushed. 'Sorry,' she said. 'That must have sounded really stupid.'

'How does sausages, bacon and scrambled eggs sound?' said Christina.

'Brilliant!' said Belinda, quickly recovering from her embarrassment.

They set about the toast and Christina brought the radio through so they could hear the news bulletin. Soon, the smells of breakfast came wafting out of the kitchen.

'This is it,' said Tracy, as the music ended and a voice announced the news. Christina stood in the kitchen doorway as the three girls listened breathlessly for a report of the aeroplane crash.

They waited anxiously as the reporter went through a number of items of local news.

'She's not going to mention it,' said Belinda.

'Shh!' said Holly.

'A single seater aeroplane crashed last night near Loch Evayne,' said the radio voice. 'Rescue teams were unable to find the pilot despite an extensive search of the area where the plane came down. Concern has been voiced that the pilot, a local businessman named as Declan Pallow, may have concussion and could have wandered into the hills. Latest news is that the rescue teams were out renewing the search at first light today.'

'The poor guy,' breathed Tracy.

'Shh!' hissed Holly. 'There's more.'

'The police are hoping that Mr Pallow will be found quickly,' continued the newsreader, 'as they want to interview him in connection with the theft of fifty thousand pounds from the offices of the property development company, Heron, Simpson and Pallow.' The three girls stared open-mouthed at one another. 'More news as it comes in,' said the woman. 'And now for the weather . . . '

'Declan Pallow,' said Christina. 'Well, I never!'

'Do you know him?' asked Holly.

'I certainly know of him,' said Christina. 'And I knew that company as well. They leafleted the whole area last year, looking to buy properties.' She gave a grim smile. 'Well, well,' she said. 'It looks as though Mr Pallow has absconded with a safe-full of the company's money. I imagine his partners are rather pleased that the plane *did* crash.'

'That news-woman didn't mention whether the money had been found, though,' said Belinda. 'You don't think it could still be on the plane, do you?'

'They'd have found it if it was,' said Holly. 'And she'd have said something about it. It must still be missing.'

'Oh, heavens! The sausages!' said Christina, disappearing into the kitchen.

'Wow!' breathed Tracy. 'What do you think happened?'

'That's easy,' said Belinda. 'He must have emptied the safe and then – into the aeroplane and *whoosh*!' She made a soaring gesture with her hand. 'Off into the wide blue yonder before anyone even knew the money was missing.' She shrugged. 'Except that he crashed.' She grinned. 'That's what my mum would call natural justice.'

'Yes, but what happened *after* he crashed?' said Holly. 'You saw the blood on the windscreen. He must have been hurt. No one could just pick themselves up and walk off after a crash like that.'

'I'd say that's exactly what he did,' said Belinda. 'He must have just grabbed the money and run – well, staggered. But I don't suppose he'll get far, not with tons of people over there searching for him.'

Holly chewed thoughtfully on a corner of toast. 'I wonder where he'd go,' she said. 'Assuming he *is* all right, I mean. He must look a bit of a state. At the very least, we know he must have cut himself in the crash.'

'Well, if I was on the run,' said Tracy, 'I'd head for the nearest way out of here. A railway station or something.'

'And where's the nearest railway station?' asked Holly.

'That must be the one we arrived at,' said Belinda. 'At Glenroch.'

47

'Is it?' asked Holly. 'Are you sure about that?'

'We'd have to look at a map,' said Tracy.

'OK,' said Holly. 'As soon as we've finished breakfast we get out a map.'

'Excuse me,' said Belinda. 'There are probably dozens of people out looking for him. People who already know the area. What's the point in us looking at a map?'

'Because,' said Holly, 'if the nearest railway station is at Glenroch, he'd have to come *this way* to get to it. He'd have to come right past here, wouldn't he?' she glanced towards the kitchen and lowered her voice. 'And we might see him. We could even try and trap him.'

'I don't think Christina would think much of that,' said Tracy.

Holly grinned. 'We don't have to tell her,' she said.

Belinda sighed. 'Here we go again,' she said.

After breakfast the three girls took a map of the local area from the pile of papers that Christina had left in the sitting-room, and went down to the beach for a discussion. But before they left the cottage, Holly ran up to her room to fetch something.

'Don't you ever go anywhere without that?' asked Belinda as she saw the Mystery Club's red notebook in Holly's hand. 'I bet you even take it in the bath with you!'

'I like to be prepared,' said Holly. 'You never know what might happen.'

They spread the map out on the sand and knelt round it.

'Here's where we are,' said Tracy, pointing to the curve in the side of Loch Evayne where Bay View Cottage was situated. 'Angel Bay.' She traced her finger down the loch to where it bent west towards the coast. 'And that's Glenroch.' They could all see the black spot that denoted the railway station. The black line of the railway curved away south in one direction, and followed the angle of the loch west in the other, heading for the coast.

'You see?' said Holly. 'He would have to come this way.' She put her finger on the map. 'He crashed there, OK? Which means he'd have to make his way right up to the end of the loch.' Her finger traced up the narrow loch and round the end. 'All the way down past Angel Bay.'

'Unless he went that way,' said Tracy, tracing her finger upwards.

'Don't be daft,' said Holly. 'That's all mountains.'

'He could be hiding out,' said Tracy. 'I bet a person could hide out for weeks up in those mountains if they didn't want to be found.'

'Yes,' said Belinda. 'And starve to death. No, Holly's right. He'd have to come this way. But, look, it's been something like fifteen hours since

49

the crash. Even if he was feeling really groggy, he'd have been able to get past here by now. Holly, what are you writing?'

'I'm just making notes of everything that's happened,' said Holly.

Their discussion was interrupted by the sound of a car approaching. Tracy stood up to see.

'Hey,' she said. 'It's the police. Come on, you guys. Maybe there's some news.'

The three girls ran up to the cottage, where a policeman was already speaking to Christina.

'Have you found him yet?' asked Holly.

The policeman shook his head. 'Not yet,' he said. 'But it's only a matter of time.'

'The money wasn't in the plane, was it?' asked Belinda.

The policeman gave her a curious look. 'I see you've been keeping up with events,' he said. 'And, no, the money wasn't found on the plane.'

'Have you got road blocks up?' asked Tracy. 'You'll need to watch all the roads round here. And you'll need to have someone watching the station. And a couple of helicopters would be a good idea. With those heat-seeking cameras, in case he's keeping under cover of the trees. We've been talking about it, and we're certain he'd have to come this way.'

The policeman looked at her in amazement. 'I think we've got the situation under control,' he said. 'I came up here to have a word with you all, as you were the first on the scene.' He took out a notepad and flipped it open. 'Would you like to tell me exactly what happened?'

'Shall we go inside?' said Christina. 'I'll make a pot of tea for us all.'

They went into the sitting-room and the policeman scribbled down notes as the three girls went over the events of the previous evening.

'Could you give us a description of him?' asked Holly, getting the Mystery Club's red notebook out again.

The policeman seemed rather taken aback as Holly poised her pen over the open notebook.

'Well, I suppose so . . . He's in his forties,' said the policeman. 'He's about two metres in height, and of slim build. Greying hair and clean shaven. We don't know what he was wearing, but he'll probably be carrying a bag.'

'With the money in it?' said Belinda.

'That's right,' said the policeman. 'It'll be a suitcase or a hold-all.'

'That's fine,' said Holly, giving the policeman a serious look. 'We'll keep our eyes open for you.'

The policeman gave her a bemused smile. 'You'll know better than to approach him if you do see him, I hope,' he said. 'A man on the run with a large amount of stolen money is not the sort of person you'd want to go anywhere near.' He looked over at Christina. 'Not that he's likely to show himself,' he said. 'The chances are, he's a good distance from here already.'

'You'll want to talk to Bobby as well,' said Holly. 'He was with us over there.'

'I've already spoken to the Talisker lad,' said the policeman. 'I had a word with him on the way here.' He looked at his notes. 'Well,' he said, 'it all seems to tie in.' He closed the notepad.

'Do you know yet why the plane crashed?' asked Holly.

'The fuel ran out,' said the policeman. 'And lucky for you it did.'

'Why's that?' asked Tracy.

The policeman shook his head. 'If that fire you put out had reached the fuel tank, and if the tank had been full of fuel and you nearby – well, I think I'd be talking to you at your hospital bedside.'

'You mean it would have exploded?' breathed Belinda.

The three girls looked at one another in horror. It had never occurred to them how much danger they had been in.

Tracy put her hands over her face. 'We could have been blown to bits!'

They were still feeling a bit stunned by what the policeman had said as they strolled a little later along the banks of the loch. The water lapped gently, lifting the rippling swathes of dark green seaweed that coated the sand beneath their feet.

'Do you think he took any notice of what we said?' asked Belinda. 'About Pallow coming this way to get to the railway station?'

'He was writing it all down,' said Holly. 'But I should think they'd have already thought of that.'

'I didn't notice him write down my suggestion about helicopters,' said Tracy. 'Or my idea about using heat-seeking cameras. Maybe they don't have sophisticated stuff like that up here?'

'You make it sound like we're a million miles from civilisation,' said Belinda. 'We're not exactly in the middle of a Brazilian jungle, you know.'

'I know,' said Tracy. 'But it is pretty remote.'

'I wonder if Bobby noticed anything else while he was on his own over there,' said Holly.

'He'll have told that policeman if he had,' said Belinda.

'Yes, of course,' said Holly. 'But we could go over to the hotel and check it out, couldn't we? I want to have the complete picture. I'm planning on writing this up for the school mag. You know, a sort of what-we-did-on-our-holidays piece. How about we take a walk down to the hotel and see if we can have a quick word with Bobby? Even if he didn't see anything else, he'll be able to tell us what happened once the rescue people arrived.'

'Can do,' said Belinda. 'But I'll tell you what I'd really like to get him to do.'

'What's that?' asked Holly.

'Tell us some more about those ospreys,' said Belinda. 'They sound really interesting. Do you think if we ask really nicely, that he'd take us back to that tree where they've got their nest? I'd love to see them.'

'We can ask,' said Holly. She smiled. 'That would make another good article for the magazine.'

'*Two* articles?' said Tracy. 'Steffie will throw a fit!'

Steffie Smith was the editor of the school magazine back in Willow Dale. She and Holly had taken a while to get used to each other, but ever since Holly and the Mystery Club had saved Steffie's brother's life, Steffie seemed a little more friendly and less bossy.

'Let's go and see Bobby right now,' said Holly. Once she had decided to do something, Holly wasn't the sort of person to put it off – as the other two members of the Mystery Club had often discovered.

They made their way back to the cottage. Christina's car was gone. Shortly after the policeman had left, she had told the three girls that she would be spending the day in Glenroch, organising her charity concert. She had taken Rosie with her, telling them not to expect her before late afternoon, and giving them the run of the kitchen to make themselves a midday meal.

'We ought to think about sending postcards home soon,' said Belinda as they walked along the pitted earth track that eventually led down to the main road. 'You know what it's like. If you don't send cards off straight away, you always end up getting home before they arrive.' She grinned at Tracy. 'And you must send one to Kurt, mustn't you, Tracy?'

'I guess so,' said Tracy. 'I'll never hear the end of it if I don't.' Kurt Welford was Tracy's part-time boyfriend back in Willow Dale.

'That's right,' said Holly. 'And I must remember to send one to Peter and Miranda.' Peter Hamilton and Miranda Hunt were old friends of Holly's from London. Before Holly had ever dreamed of the adventures she was to have with Belinda and Tracy, she and her two old friends had teamed up in London as the Mystery Kids. They had only been twelve at the time, but that hadn't stopped them getting involved in plenty of adventures of their own.

'Keep your eyes peeled,' said Holly. 'Declan Pallow might still be lurking round here somewhere.'

The path moved away from the reedy loch-side and entered a stretch of woodland.

'You know what we really need?' said Tracy. 'Some sort of pocket transmitters – like the police

55

have. That way we'd be able to spread out and keep in contact with one another.'

'Wouldn't that be a bit expensive?' said Holly. 'The most I could afford would be two tin cans and a bit of string.'

Tracy looked at her. 'Tin cans?' she said. 'What for?'

'Don't you know about that?' said Holly. 'You knot the string through a hole in the bottom of the cans, and then, if you keep the string tight, you can talk to each other.'

'You're kidding?' said Tracy.

'No,' said Holly. 'It works. Honestly.'

Holly stopped suddenly, her hand lifted towards the others as she listened. It had only been a small noise. A rustling in the trees over to their right.

'What?' said Belinda.

'Quiet,' breathed Holly, stepping off the path and listening intently. 'I heard something.'

'I can't hear anything,' whispered Tracy. 'Holly, you're imagining things again.'

Holly shook her head and walked a little further into the trees, pushing the tangled bushes aside and listening again. Her hand grabbed Belinda's arm and she pointed.

Something dark was moving through the trees and bushes. Something large enough to be a man – although all they could see were patches of darkness through the mass of undergrowth; brief snatches of something that could be a jacket or a dark coat.

Holly took another step forwards, but Belinda caught hold of her and pulled her back on to the path.

'What are you doing?' whispered Holly. 'That could be *him*!'

'You heard what the policeman said,' Belinda reminded her. 'We shouldn't approach him. If it is him, the last thing we want to do is go chasing him through the woods. We should go and tell someone.'

'And let him get away?' said Holly. 'Not on your life! Look, the hotel can't be far away. You two go and get help. I'll stay here and watch.'

'Don't do anything dumb,' said Tracy.

'I won't,' said Holly. 'I'm just going to keep watch, OK? I'll stay right here.'

The two girls looked uncertainly at her for a moment, and then Belinda nodded.

Holly watched as her two friends trotted down the path towards the side road that led to the hotel.

The woods were strangely silent. Holly remembered her promise not to go in after the man, but it was impossible for her just to stand there.

What if it really were Declan Pallow? What if he managed to slip away unobserved while she was waiting?

With a last glance along the path where her friends had gone, Holly stepped again into the trees. No harm could come to her, she reasoned, not so long as she kept herself perfectly quiet and didn't go too near the man.

She crept through the trees, holding her breath, her ears straining for any sound, her eyes alert for any sign of movement. It had been a man that she had seen. She was certain of it.

She glimpsed the figure again, moving through the trees several metres away from her. She caught her breath. Branches and leaves screened the figure, breaking the shape up. But this time she saw a dark blue anorak with a distinctive orange stripe across the shoulders, and the fleeting sight of grey hair. Grey hair! The policeman had said that Declan Pallow had grey hair!

Holly kept perfectly still. The last thing she wanted was to be seen by the man. She grimaced in uncertainty as the figure moved away from her. What should she do? Follow and risk being caught, or wait there and risk losing him?

She let out an annoyed breath as the man vanished into the trees. There was really no choice; she had to follow him. Wincing at every crackle that her feet made on the ground, she crept in pursuit.

She tensed, hearing a movement away to her

left. The movement became a crashing through the trees and Holly threw her arms up to protect herself as a dark shape came bursting towards her.

5 Suspicions

Belinda was out of breath within two minutes of leaving Holly, and Tracy was slowly pulling ahead of her as they jogged along the path. The turn-off for the hotel was further away than they had expected. Driving along here in a car, the distances had not seemed so great.

'Come on,' said Tracy, glancing round at her.

'I can't run any faster,' panted Belinda. 'If I'd known we were going to be doing all this racing around, I'd have brought Meltdown with me!' Meltdown was Belinda's greatest love – her chestnut thoroughbred.

'It can't be far now,' said Tracy. 'We can't waste any time. You know what Holly's like. She'll be in there after him if we're not quick.'

'If it is him,' gasped Belinda, putting on a spurt to catch up with Tracy. 'I still think Pallow will be miles away by now. Oh, thank heavens; here we are!'

They came to the side road and saw the roof of the Angel Hotel in the distance.

The road curved between unkempt lawns and spread itself out into a wide area in front of the hotel where several cars were parked.

'Bobby!' shouted Tracy. 'There's Bobby!'

The boy was at the side of the hotel, lifting a black rubbish sack into a large dustbin.

'Hello? What's going on?' he asked as the two girls came running up to him.

'We think we've seen him,' said Tracy, pointing back the way they'd come. 'Back there – in the woods.'

'Seen who?' asked Bobby.

'Declan Pallow!' said Tracy. 'The man from the plane.'

'Get away,' said Bobby. 'He'll be long gone.'

'That's what I think,' panted Belinda. 'But we saw *someone*. And Holly's back there keeping watch.'

'It won't be Pallow,' said Bobby.

'You don't know that!' exclaimed Tracy.

Bobby looked uncertainly at them for a few moments.

'OK,' he said. 'Show me where you saw him. And if it does turn out to be Pallow, we'll come straight back here and phone the police.'

'Oh, crumbs!' Belinda panted as Tracy and Bobby ran back the way they had come. 'I'm going to need a holiday after all this!'

She chased after them, back down the side road and in through the trees again.

'Wait!' she shouted after they had been running for a couple of minutes. 'It was here!'

The other two stopped and looked round at her.

'It was,' she said. 'I recognise it. Holly must have got fed up with waiting for us. She must have gone in after him.'

'Oh, no,' said Tracy. 'We told her to wait! Are you sure it was here?'

'I'm certain,' said Belinda, diving off the track and pushing her way through the branches.

The three of them fought their way through the woods, searching for their missing friend.

Holly picked herself up. She didn't know who had been more startled – her or the deer. It had broken out of cover only a couple of metres away from her. She had caught a flash of wide brown eyes and a streak of tan-coloured hide as the deer had jinked away from her and gone speeding away through the trees. The shock had caught her off balance and she had fallen with a yell as the sound of the fleeing animal had faded away.

It was only a deer, you idiot, she said to herself. But she was still trembling from the surprise encounter. Under any other circumstances she would have been delighted to have come so close to a deer. But with her nerves strained by the thought of the runaway thief lurking nearby, the sudden appearance of the animal had left her feeling quite weak-kneed.

She took a few steadying breaths and looked round. If the man Pallow was nearby, he couldn't have failed to have heard all that noise, not to mention her yell. So much for creeping up on him!

'I might as well go back,' she sighed. She had retraced her steps about halfway to the path when she saw flashes of colour ahead.

Belinda's face appeared, red from running.

'Got you!' said Belinda. 'You were supposed to stay on the path!'

'I know,' said Holly as Tracy and Bobby came up to her.

'Have you seen him again?' asked Tracy.

'Yes,' said Holly. 'And I'm pretty sure it was him. I saw grey hair.' She gave them a rueful look. 'But then I lost him. And I almost got mown down by a deer. It nearly knocked me over.'

'A deer!' said Belinda. 'Are you sure it wasn't a deer you saw all along?'

'Of course it wasn't,' said Holly. 'I told you – I saw him! He was wearing a dark blue jacket – and he had grey hair.'

'It could have been anyone,' said Bobby. 'I'll bet you it wasn't Declan Pallow. It'll have been someone taking a ramble.'

'That's exactly what I thought,' said Belinda.

She looked at Bobby. 'Holly's got a very vivid imagination.'

The four of them came out onto the path.

'Are we going to fetch the police?' asked Holly.

'What? Because you think you saw someone who might have been Declan Pallow?' said Belinda. 'Bobby's probably right – it'll be some innocent holidaymaker out for a walk.'

'I think she's right,' said Bobby. 'The policeman I spoke to this morning said they were convinced he'd be a long way from here by now.'

Holly looked at her friends, seeing the doubt on their faces.

'Is anyone prepared to come and look for him again with me?' she asked.

Belinda looked into the trees. 'I'd rather not,' she said. Tracy nodded in agreement.

'OK,' Holly said reluctantly. 'But you're going to feel pretty silly if it turns out it was him.'

'Believe me,' said Bobby. 'Plenty of people wander through these woods in the summer. It's probably someone from the hotel.'

'Hmm,' said Holly. 'If you say so.' She was unconvinced, but she didn't want to go searching on her own.

'Did you hear about the stolen money?' Tracy asked Bobby.

'Yes,' he said, 'it was on the radio. Have the police been to see you yet?'

Holly nodded. 'We told him everything we saw,' she said. 'Did you tell him what happened after we left? When you were on your own over there?'

Bobby gave her a strange look. 'What do you mean?' he asked. 'Nothing happened. I don't know what you're talking about.'

Holly was surprised by the defensive tone in Bobby's voice. It was almost as if he thought she was accusing him of something.

'I meant when the rescue people arrived,' said Holly. 'What did you think I meant?'

'Oh!' Bobby's expression changed in an instant. He smiled and shrugged. 'They got there a few minutes after you'd all gone,' he said. 'I stayed there while they searched round the place, then they gave me a lift back.'

'Did they look in the plane?' asked Tracy.

'No,' said Bobby. 'Why?'

'For the money,' said Tracy.

'I don't think they knew anything about the stolen money at the time,' said Bobby. 'Anyway – there was nothing in there.'

'How do you know that?' asked Belinda.

'I had a look,' said Bobby. 'Just to see if there was anything to give them some idea of who the pilot was. There was nothing in there at all. I think I'd have spotted a suitcase big enough to take fifty thousand pounds.'

'So he must have taken it with him,' said Holly.

'Of course he did,' said Bobby. 'And that's why he didn't want to be found.' He looked at his watch. 'I'd better be getting back to the hotel,' he said. 'I get in enough trouble over there for all the time I take off to watch over the ospreys, without disappearing on wild manhunts.'

'Do you think you could tell us some more about the ospreys some time?' asked Belinda. 'I'd love to see them. And we wouldn't tell anyone where their nest was.'

'I don't see why not,' said Bobby. 'I'll tell you what – I'm working all day today, but why don't I come up to the cottage tomorrow morning? You might even get to see them in flight.'

'That would be wonderful,' said Holly.

'It's a date,' said Bobby. 'And bring field glasses, if you've got any.'

The three girls went back to the cottage and discussed their plans for the rest of the day.

'Why don't we explore along the loch?' suggested Holly. 'We could make some sandwiches and have a picnic.'

'On one condition,' said Belinda. 'We don't spend all our time on the lookout for Declan Pallow. I've done enough running around recently to last me a lifetime.'

'Don't go on about that,' said Holly. 'I did see a man in the woods.'

'Yeah, right,' said Tracy. 'A guy with antlers and fur.' Holly glared at her. 'All right,' said Tracy. 'So it was a man. But, like Bobby said, it could have been anyone.' She looked in the fridge. 'Ew! What's *this*?'

Belinda leaned over her shoulder. 'It's a haggis,' she said, taking the plate out and showing the round, brown haggis to Holly. 'Anyone for haggis sandwiches?'

'You can't eat haggis in a sandwich, surely?' said Holly.

'I was joking,' said Belinda. 'Christina must have wanted to give us a Scottish treat.'

'What's it made out of?' asked Tracy, eying it dubiously.

'Liver, lungs and heart, all minced up with onions and oats, and stuff like that,' said Belinda. 'Then they put it in a sheep's stomach. It's supposed to be really nice.'

'Yeah,' said Tracy. 'I bet it tastes as good as it sounds! Forget it!'

Belinda laughed and put the haggis back. They made themselves a big pile of sandwiches – but none with haggis in.

'Shall we take field glasses with us?' said Holly. 'You never know – we might catch sight of the ospreys. And even if we don't, there's bound to be other things to look at.'

They set off northwards along the shore of the loch.

'It'll be great if we get to see the ospreys,' said Tracy. 'Bobby seems a really nice guy. And I bet he knows his way all over this area. Maybe he'll even take us over to the mountains one day, if he can get time off.'

'You're determined to get up those mountains, aren't you?' said Belinda.

'I'll say!' said Tracy. She pointed to the far mountain tops across the loch. 'Right up there!' she said. 'To the very peak!'

'Don't you think there was something strange in the way Bobby reacted when I asked him what went on after we'd come back to the cottage last night?' Holly said thoughtfully.

'What sort of strange?' asked Belinda.

'I'm not sure,' said Holly. 'But I know what it reminded me of: Jamie.' Jamie was Holly's mischievous younger brother. 'It was like when something has been broken at home, and Mum asks Jamie if he knows anything about it. Before he'll own up, he goes into this big innocent act. The way Bobby behaved when I asked him about what happened while he was on his own over there was *exactly* the same. You know – really defensive.'

Belinda looked at Tracy. 'I think the Adams imagination is over-heating again,' she said.

'Well . . . maybe,' said Holly. She smiled at her friends. 'Yes, I expect you're right. I'm just getting suspicious about nothing.'

The sun was high overhead as they found themselves a quiet place to have their picnic. Tracy gathered flat stones and went down to the water's edge to skip them.

'Whoo!' she said. 'Five bounces!' as one of her stones went leaping out across the water. 'I bet no one can beat that!'

'Easy!' said Belinda. 'Let me show you how it's really done.'

Holly watched her two friends skipping stones out across the loch for a while. She still couldn't clear her mind of the nagging feeling that something had happened while Bobby had been alone with the aeroplane wreck.

After a while she climbed up the beach and found herself a ridge of tufted grass to sit on. She took her field glasses out of their case and swept them across the far side of the loch. The trees leaped up to her eyes; dense and dark and still in the warm afternoon air. She roved the magnified circle along the far shore, the yelling and laughing of her two friends loud in her ears as they competed to skip the stones as far as they could.

A movement caught her attention as she swept the field glasses to and fro. A figure came out of the trees and moved down the beach, very close to where the aeroplane had come down. Holly turned the focusing wheel, trying to get a clearer image, but the picture only became more blurred, and even that small movement sent the circle of magnification skidding away from the figure.

By the time she found it again, the tiny figure was moving rapidly back into the trees. But there was something different about it.

'Hey!' she called. 'Quick! Come up here!'

'What is it?' called Belinda.

'There's someone over there,' said Holly. 'Near where the aeroplane crashed.'

'It'll be one of the search team,' said Tracy.

The two girls scrambled up to where Holly was sitting, but by the time Holly had handed over the field glasses for Tracy to look, the far shore of the loch was empty again.

'I suppose you think it was Declan Pallow, do you?' said Belinda. 'Holly, this is getting silly!'

'I never said I thought it was him,' said Holly. 'But someone went down to the water and then back into the trees. And I'm sure he was carrying something on the way down – and that he didn't have it on the way back.'

'Ooh!' said Belinda, mockingly. 'What was it, Holly? A dead body?'

'No. It was like a bag or a sack.' She looked at her friends. 'I did see it, honestly.'

'Give me those glasses,' said Belinda. She spent a few moments scanning the far bank. 'There's nothing there,' she said. 'Tracy? Do you fancy swimming across to see if Holly's right?'

'No thanks,' said Tracy. 'Look, forget it, Holly. When will you get it into your head that the guy has gone? He'd have been found if he was still hanging around. Are you going to spend the whole of the rest of this week freaking out every time you see someone?'

'I don't like mysteries,' said Holly. 'And the way Declan Pallow has just vanished is very mysterious.'

'You don't like mysteries?' said Belinda with a laugh. 'You're joking!'

'I mean I don't like *unsolved* mysteries,' said Holly. 'And I don't care what either of you says. Until I hear that the police have found him, I'm going to keep my eyes open. I don't believe Declan Pallow has gone, like everyone's saying. I think he's still here somewhere.'

'Why do you think that?' asked Tracy. 'Don't you think he'd have been caught by now?'

'Not if he was hiding out somewhere,' said Holly. 'What would you do if you were being hunted down? And don't forget he's hurt – remember the blood? If I'd just staggered out of a crashed plane, and I knew people would be hunting for me, I wouldn't run for it. I'd find somewhere to hide. A cave or something. And I'd stay there until I thought it was safe to get away.'

Holly stared out across the loch. She didn't care what anyone said. She was convinced that Declan

Pallow was over there somewhere, licking his wounds and waiting for the hunt to be called off.

'You can't have it both ways,' said Belinda. 'Either Pallow is hiding over there, or he's lurking in the woods over *here*. He can't be in both places at once.' She looked at Tracy. 'And, if you ask me, he isn t in either place.'

Holly ignored her. 'I wonder if there are caves over there?' said Holly. 'I bet Bobby would know.'

'You can ask him tomorrow,' said Belinda. 'And anyway, if there are, don't you think the people searching for Pallow would have thought of it?'

'Not necessarily,' persisted Holly. 'Not if they were looking for someone who they thought was trying to get *away* from the area.' She stood up. 'I'm going back to the hotel to speak to Bobby. Tomorrow might be too late.'

'Oh, Holly!' sighed Belinda.

'It's OK,' said Holly. 'You two don't have to come with me. I'll meet you back here in a while.'

Holly's inquisitive nature wouldn't allow her to relax and enjoy herself while there was a mystery to be solved. And what if, in a couple of days, a cave were found with signs that Declan Pallow had been there and had gone?

She walked briskly back to the hotel, already half-convinced that her theory was right.

She walked up the broad steps to the front

entrance. The foyer was deserted, but there was a reception desk with a bell. She rang and waited.

After a minute or two a young woman in a smart black suit emerged from a side door.

'I'm sorry to bother you,' said Holly. 'But would it be possible for me to have a quick word with Bobby Talisker? I think he works in the kitchens.'

'He's not here,' said the woman. 'He went home with a headache a few hours ago.'

'Oh!' That was odd. A few hours ago they had been talking to Bobby, and he hadn't mentioned a headache.

'Between you and me,' said the woman, glancing round and leaning over the desk, 'I think he was faking it. But I wouldn't say as much to the owners. If you ask me, he's skived off to watch those silly birds of his.' She shook her head. 'He'll get caught one day. I've warned him often enough.'

'Thanks, anyway,' said Holly.

She came out of the hotel, her forehead furrowed in thought. Bobby must have used his headache excuse almost immediately after he had left them that morning.

But if he was pretending to be ill so he could go and check on the birds, why hadn't he taken the girls along with him? He knew they wanted to see the ospreys.

Once again, Holly found herself harbouring puzzled suspicions about Bobby. If he hadn't gone to look at the ospreys, then where *had* he gone? And why?

6   Fishing for clues

Holly told her two friends about Bobby's curious disappearance when she met up with them later that afternoon, but neither of them seemed to think there was anything particularly strange about it.

'You never know,' said Belinda as she munched her way through the last of their sandwiches. 'Perhaps he did come to the cottage, and we were already gone. Anyway, you can ask him about it tomorrow.'

They spent the rest of the afternoon rambling along the lochside. Christina was back at the cottage by the time they arrived there, and all other thoughts were banished by the delicious smell of cooking that met them at the door.

In the evening, the four of them went down on to the beach to play ball with Rosie, and for a while Holly forgot her suspicions as she joined in with the fun.

'I've managed to get a free day later in the week,' said Christina. 'So if the three of you would like to choose some places to visit, I'd

77

be more than happy to take you out for the day.'

'I'd love to go up on the mountains,' said Tracy.

Christina smiled. 'I didn't quite mean that,' she said. 'I thought I could take you for a drive. There's a sea-life sanctuary along the coast. You might see some seals, if you're lucky.'

'Seals?' said Holly. 'Do seals ever come into the loch?'

'Not very often,' said Christina. 'But we do get other things drifting in here sometimes.'

'Sharks?' asked Belinda.

Christina laughed. 'No, not sharks, thankfully. These waters are usually too cold for sharks. But we get jellyfish. In fact, at this time of year, we get one of the biggest jellyfish there is. It's called a lion's mane. You should watch out for those. They can give you a nasty sting. And you'll probably see a few moonjellies, too.'

'Are they dangerous?' asked Belinda, already staring nervously out across the water, half-expecting to see the spooky translucent jellyfish bubbles drifting menacingly on the surface.

'That depends what you mean by dangerous,' said Christina. 'They can give you a nasty sting. It's best not to touch any you might find washed up.' She smiled. 'I did hear that one was washed up near here that was nearly twenty metres long.'

78

She laughed. 'You wouldn't want to get tangled up with *that*, would you?'

'No, I wouldn't,' said Belinda with a shudder. 'I hate things like that.'

It wasn't long before the girls were yawning.

'Oh, excuse me,' said Tracy, covering her mouth with her hand. 'It must be all this fresh air.'

'You won't have any trouble getting off to sleep tonight,' said Christina. 'Shall we go back for a bit of supper? You could write some postcards. I'm sure your parents will want to know how you're getting along.'

Mrs McKetchnie had a supply of postcards at the cottage, and while the girls were eating their supper, they wrote holiday messages home.

'I'm doing a special one for Jamie,' said Holly. '"Having a wonderful time. Glad you're not here."'

'That's not very kind,' said Belinda.

'You're kidding?' said Holly. 'That's exactly what he put on the card he sent to me when he went on that school trip to France a few months back.'

'Leave the cards on the table by the door,' said Christina. 'I'll post them in Glenroch tomorrow.'

As she settled into bed, Holly found her thoughts going back to Bobby Talisker. Were her friends right? Was she just being over-suspicious?

Oh well, she thought drowsily, *I expect it'll all be explained in the morning.*

*   *   *

79

It was about half past nine the following morning, and the three girls were having a good-natured argument about where they would like Christina to take them later in the week.

'Loch Ness is only about ninety kilometres north of here,' said Tracy. 'Maybe Christina will drive us up for a look at the monster?'

'I'd rather see the seals in the sea-life sanctuary,' said Holly. 'At least we know they exist.'

'What about this?' said Belinda, waving a leaflet. 'There's a working farm not very far away. They might have some horses.'

Holly laughed. 'At this rate, Christina is going to be driving us all over Scotland. I want to see seals, you want to see some horses, and Tracy's desperate to see the Loch Ness monster.'

There was a rap at the window and they looked round to see Bobby waving in at them.

'Are you all set for a look at our ospreys?' he asked as they went out to meet him.

'We certainly are,' said Holly. 'And I've got my field glasses.'

They set off towards the woods.

'Did you see them yesterday afternoon?' Holly asked Bobby.

'No,' said Bobby. 'I was working.'

'You were?' said Tracy. She looked at Holly. 'But Holly went to the hotel yesterday afternoon, and they said you'd gone home.'

Holly thought she saw a flicker of unease pass across Bobby's face. 'I was there all day,' he said. 'What time was this?'

'I'm not sure,' said Holly. 'Mid-afternoon.'

'Oh, I know,' said Bobby. 'My boss sent me out to get some stuff. You must have turned up while I was gone.'

'But they said you weren't well,' said Holly. 'I was told you'd gone home with a headache.'

'Who did you speak to?' asked Bobby.

'A woman at the reception desk,' said Holly. 'With long black hair.'

'Oh, you mean Helen,' said Bobby. He shook his head. 'You can't take any notice of her. She doesn't know what's going on half the time. You should have spoken to Mr Williamson – he knew where I was.' He smiled, and once again Holly was reminded of her younger brother. 'What did you want?'

'She thinks Declan Pallow is lurking in a cave up on the mountains,' said Belinda. 'She thinks he's lying low until the search is called off.'

'It's a reasonable theory,' said Holly. She looked at Bobby. 'Are there any caves over there?'

'None that I know of,' said Bobby. 'And he wouldn't still be there, if there were. He'd have waited until nightfall and then scarpered.'

'I saw someone over there yesterday afternoon,' said Holly. 'Someone came out of the trees and down to the water. And I'm sure they dropped something in the loch.'

'You must have very good eyes,' said Bobby. 'I'm sure I couldn't have seen anything at that distance.'

'I was looking through my field glasses,' said Holly. 'Would it be possible for us to walk there? Right round the end of the loch? I'd like to have a closer look.'

'It's possible,' said Bobby. 'But it will take a couple of hours in each direction. I thought you wanted to see the ospreys.'

'We do,' said Belinda. 'Take no notice of Holly. She's got a bee in her bonnet about Declan Pallow.' She grinned. 'I think she's hoping to catch him all by herself and claim the reward money.'

'I am not!' exclaimed Holly. 'I never even thought about that!'

Bobby looked sharply at her. 'Have you heard something?' he asked. 'Something about a reward?'

'No, of course not,' said Holly. 'Belinda's just being funny.'

'But there would be a reward, wouldn't there?' said Bobby. 'I mean – if someone found the money?'

'I suppose there might be,' said Holly.

'Sure there will,' said Tracy.

Bobby looked at her. 'How much, do you think?' he asked. 'Something like ten per cent, maybe?'

Tracy shrugged. 'I guess it could be as much as that.' Her eyes lit up. 'Hey! That would be five thousand pounds!' She grinned at Holly. 'Maybe we *should* be searching for that guy. I can think of a lot of things I could do with five thousand pounds.'

Holly thought Bobby was oddly quiet after that. And she still wasn't convinced by his explanation about the previous afternoon. She said nothing, but a suspicion was growing in her that Bobby had some secret that he wasn't telling them. And the more she thought about it, the more certain she became that it was something to do with Declan Pallow and the stolen money.

'Isn't the tree where they've got their nest over there?' asked Tracy, pointing into the woods where they had got lost on that first afternoon.

'It is,' said Bobby. 'But I'm not taking you there. If we're lucky, we'll see something a lot more interesting from where we're going.'

He led them to a high ridge overlooking the loch.

'How are you at being patient?' he said. 'We might have to wait some time. If he comes at all.'

'If who comes?' asked Tracy, looking round. 'Have you arranged to meet someone here?'

'Not someone,' said Bobby, sitting down. 'Some *thing*. We're on the direct flight line from the nest to the loch. We may have already missed it, but if we're lucky, we might get to see the male bird doing some fishing. I often sit up here to watch him catch fish. It's the most amazing thing you've ever seen.'

They sat down with him, taking it in turns to scan the trees for a sign of the bird.

'What exactly do they look like?' asked Belinda.

'In flight they look a bit like big gulls,' said Bobby. 'They're mostly white underneath, but they've got much longer wings, with ragged edges. A bit like a buzzard.'

'That would help if I knew what a buzzard looked like,' said Belinda. She took a sudden breath and let out a yell. 'I see it!' she shouted, as a large shape lifted out of the trees and swept through the air above their heads.

The bird swung low over the loch as the three girls gazed in awe. It tilted and they saw the brown of its wings.

Three or four times it circled out over the loch.

'It's beautiful,' said Tracy. 'Oh! Why didn't I bring my camera!'

The glorious bird suddenly swooped. They could see its talons outstretched as it dived low over the water.

It was all over in a second. There was hardly a splash as the bird soared into the sky, a fish struggling in his talons. As the osprey headed back to its nest they heard a faint 'pew!' cry, and then it was gone.

'That was amazing,' said Holly.

'They're wonderful creatures,' said Bobby. 'I just wish I didn't have to work in that hotel every day. I'd like to spend all my time keeping watch over them. They come up from Africa in April, and they're here right through the summer. If only I had— ' He stopped speaking and frowned. Holly looked at him. It was almost as if he had been about to say something, but had thought better of it.

He looked at his watch. 'I'd better be getting back soon,' he said. 'I'm working this afternoon.'

'Will he come for some more fish?' asked Tracy.

'Maybe,' said Bobby. 'It's worth waiting.' He looked at Holly. 'I think you'd enjoy this more than that long walk round the loch,' he said. 'If I were you, I'd forget all about Declan Pallow. He's long gone.'

After Bobby had left, the three friends sat for a while, hoping to see the osprey again. But Holly's mind was on other things.

'There's something Bobby's not telling us,' she said. 'Something to do with the crash, or the money. He knows something, I'm sure of it.' She looked hopefully at her friends. 'Let's go over there. Over to the place where the aeroplane crashed. Maybe we'll find some clues.'

'It's a two hour walk,' said Belinda. 'Bobby told us that.'

'Oh, come on,' said Tracy. 'It's a nice day. A long walk will do us good.' She looked at Belinda. 'And you know we won't have any peace until Holly gets her way.'

That settled it. Despite some grumbled protests from Belinda, the three of them set off on the long journey round the far end of the loch.

Even Belinda had to admit that the scenery was worth the effort, and it was easy enough to follow the earth path that wound up to the tip of the loch.

'We should have brought something to eat,' mumbled Belinda as they rounded the broad tip of the loch and started to walk down the far side – the side that Holly had been observing through her field glasses. 'I don't suppose there are any cafés hidden round here?'

'I doubt it,' said Tracy with a laugh. 'You could always try catching a fish.'

The path headed upwards along the slope of the hillside, cutting its way through the trees.

'I wonder where that goes,' said Holly.

'Christina mentioned a place called Iron Stone Croft,' said Tracy. 'I suppose it must go there. I can't see any buildings, though.'

'No,' said Holly. 'And we don't want to go up there, anyway.' She led the way down to the shore

86

of the loch. Banks of seaweed lay along the water's edge. The three girls walked along the gravelly sand with a cool breeze in their faces.

The loch bent in a series of small bays and as they came to one of the headlands they saw the distant figure of a man standing at the water's edge. Even from that far away, they could see that he was holding a fishing rod.

Tracy grinned at Belinda. 'Maybe he'll let you have a fish, if you ask nicely,' she said. 'Then all we'd need to do is make up a little campfire and we could have grilled fish for lunch. How does that sound?'

'Great,' Belinda said longingly. 'And how would we make a fire? By striking sparks off your head?'

The loch dipped into another bay and by the time they were in a position to see the man again, he was gone.

'Where did he go?' wondered Holly.

'Up into the trees, I suppose,' said Belinda. 'Perhaps he's staying at that Iron Stone Croft place.'

But something caught Holly's attention as they came to the spot where the man had been standing. The damp stretch of seaweed had been disturbed, and strips of seaweed had been pulled up the beach, as though something had been taken out of the loch. And the sand showed signs of something having been dragged across it – a clear trail that led up to the trees.

'What did I tell you?' said Holly. 'I *knew* someone had thrown something in the loch. That man must have just pulled it out again.'

A shallow furrow, about half a metre wide, had been scored in the sand. Holly followed it up the beach. A steep, narrow path of beaten earth wound up into the trees. The sort of path made by the passage of feet over a long period. Holly picked up a strand of seaweed and showed it to her friends.

'He must have dragged whatever it was up here,' she said.

'So let's find out where this goes,' said Tracy.

The three of them scrambled up the steep path. Exposed tree roots and stones made rough steps as the path zigzagged its way up through the woods.

'It meets the road,' said Tracy, as she emerged from the trees. The earth track that they had been following round the loch lay across their path.

'And look at this,' said Holly. There was more seaweed on the road. But there was no sign of the fisherman, nor any indication of which way he had gone.

'He must have put whatever it was down here,' said Belinda, looking closely at the seaweed remains. 'He put it down, cleaned the rest of the weed off – aha!'

'What?' asked Holly, leaning over her.

'See this?' said Belinda, pointing to a clump

of seaweed that had been crushed into the dirt. 'Something heavy had gone over this.'

'Maybe he stepped on it,' said Tracy.

'I don't think so,' said Belinda. 'It's flattened right into the road.' She looked up at her friends. 'I'd say it was a car.' She stood up. 'OK,' she said, 'let's work this out. He fishes something out of the loch, right? Then he drags it up here.' She pointed to the seaweed. 'He puts it down and cleans it off— '

'And then he puts it in the car and drives away,' interrupted Holly.

'Yeah, great,' said Tracy. 'But what was it?'

The sound of movement in the trees made them all look round.

'I think I can explain that,' said Bobby, stepping from behind a tree. He gave them a downcast look. 'It was the money from the aeroplane.'

7 Bobby's secret

'I think you'd better tell us all about it,' said Holly as Bobby stepped out on to the path.

'I never meant to keep the money,' said Bobby, looking anxiously at the three girls. 'You've got to believe that. I'm not a thief.'

'You found it in the plane, didn't you?' said Holly.

'Yes,' said Bobby. 'But I was only doing what I told you; I was just looking for something that might identify the pilot. I found the suitcase tucked down behind the pilot's seat. The key was in the lock, so I opened it to see what was inside.' His eyes took on a haunted look. 'I've never seen so much money in all my life,' he breathed. 'All neatly packed away in there. I could see that it had to be *thousands* of pounds.'

'Fifty thousand pounds, to be exact,' said Belinda.

Bobby looked at the accusing eyes of the three girls.

'So why didn't you hand it over to the rescue people?' asked Holly.

'I was going to, of course,' said Bobby. 'And then I thought, maybe there would be a reward.' He looked at Belinda. 'Like you said, you know?' He squirmed uneasily as they looked at him. 'I was going to give it back,' he said. 'But I thought that if the money just vanished for a while, the reward might go up. So I locked the case again and hid it in the undergrowth. I was going to leave it a day or two, and then pretend I'd found it on my own.'

'And take any reward just for yourself!' exclaimed Tracy.

'No, not for myself,' said Bobby. 'For a bird sanctuary. I'm a member of the local bird-watchers club. We've been trying to raise the money to set up a proper sanctuary in the area for ages. Didn't Mrs McKetchnie tell you about it? She's organising a concert for the same reason. We want to buy the woodland where the ospreys have got their nest. *That's* why I wanted to get the reward money. It wasn't for me!'

'Is that true?' asked Belinda. 'You've been telling us lies all along. Why should we believe you now?'

'If you don't believe me, ask Mrs McKetchnie,' said Bobby.

'We will, don't you worry,' said Belinda. 'But I still don't follow this. If you took the money on the night of the crash, who was it that Holly saw hiding it by the loch yesterday?'

'It was you, wasn't it?' said Holly, looking at Bobby. 'What was the idea? Were you afraid someone might find it?'

Bobby nodded. 'I hid the case in the undergrowth originally. But then, when I found out how much money there was – and that the police were involved – I thought I'd better find somewhere safer to hide it. But only until I was sure there was a reward. I'd have handed it over straight away, then.'

'That doesn't explain what you're doing here now,' said Tracy. 'Were you following us?'

'No,' said Bobby. 'I hoped you'd stay where I left you earlier.'

'I get it,' said Belinda. 'You realised Holly had seen you hiding the case by the loch.'

'That's right,' said Bobby. 'And when Holly said she wanted to come over here, I knew I had to move the case again.'

'But you had a head start on us,' said Tracy. 'You'd have had plenty of time to move the case before we arrived.'

'I had to keep off the road,' said Bobby. 'You still had those field glasses. I didn't want to risk you seeing me.' He looked at them. 'It takes a lot longer when you're walking through the woods.'

'But why did you put the case in the loch?' asked Belinda. 'The money could have got soaked. Or the whole thing could have just floated away.'

'I put it in a plastic sack,' said Bobby. 'And I hid it under the seaweed – weighted down with stones. I didn't think anyone would be able to find it.'

'Well, someone did,' said Tracy.

'I know,' said Bobby. 'I was in the trees when I saw you. And I heard you say that something had been taken out of the loch.' He sighed again. 'It didn't take a genius to guess what it was.'

'So you didn't see who took it?' asked Belinda.

Bobby shook his head. 'Did you?'

'Only from a long way off,' said Holly. 'He was fishing when we spotted him. He must have caught his line on it, or something. By the time we got there, he was gone.'

'And the money with him,' said Tracy with a low whistle.

'It serves you right,' said Belinda. 'You should have handed that money over straight away. You won't see any reward now. That man has probably taken it straight off to the police – like you should have done.'

'And the police are going to want to know how the money came to be hidden away like that,' said Holly.

'I'll say they will,' said Tracy. 'And it won't take them long to figure out who did it. I think you're in big trouble, Bobby.'

'Do you think they'll believe I didn't mean to keep the money?' Bobby asked anxiously.

'They might,' said Holly. 'If you go straight to the police station and tell them everything.'

'I've been really stupid, haven't I?' said Bobby. 'I should have given the money over straight away. But you're right; I've got to tell the police about it.'

'We'll come with you, if you like,' said Holly.

Bobby hesitated for a few moments, staring at the ground and gnawing his lip.

'OK,' he said, looking at them. 'I'll go to the police. But we don't have to walk back round the loch. There's a rowing-boat tied up at a landing place not far from here. We can row across. I'll take the boat back later.'

He led them along the road to where a steeply-shelved stairway of uneven stones made its way down through the trees.

'The boat belongs to Gregory Fox, the man who lives in Iron Stone Croft,' he told them. 'I don't think he uses it all that often. He's pretty much a recluse. He lives all on his own up there.' He turned just as he was about to go down the steps. 'You can just see the chimney of the croft.'

They followed the line of his gaze. The uppermost rim of a chimney was just visible through the trees.

'Talk about isolated,' said Belinda. 'Are there any other houses round here?'

'No,' said Bobby. 'I think he likes it that way. He's a bit strange.'

'Maybe he was the one who found the case?' said Tracy. 'I mean, there can't be all that many people round here.'

'I don't know,' said Bobby. 'What did the man you saw look like?'

'We didn't see much,' said Holly. 'But I think he was quite old. He had grey hair and a grey beard – I saw that much.'

'That's not Gregory Fox,' said Bobby. 'He's much younger than that. But quite a few people come over here for the fishing. It was probably a holidaymaker.'

They came out on to the beach. A small, ramshackle wooden jetty stretched a couple of metres into the water, looking very much the worse for wear, with rotten timbers and missing planks.

'Well?' said Belinda. 'Where's this boat, then?'

Bobby frowned. 'It's usually here,' he said. 'Tied up by the jetty.'

They looked out across the loch. A hundred metres away, the steep sides of Innis Maer rose out of the still water. But there was no sign of anyone in a boat.

'It looks like we'll be walking, then,' said Belinda. She looked at Bobby. 'You know what you could do with round here?' she said. 'Some decent public transport!'

* * *

Even Tracy was footsore and worn out by the time they arrived back at Angel Bay. The sun was resting on the mountain-tops and a chill breeze ruffled their hair.

'Christina's back,' said Tracy as they neared the cottage and saw the car parked outside. 'She'll be able to give us a lift into Glenroch.'

'No,' said Bobby. 'I want to go on my own. It's going to be bad enough explaining it all to the police, without having to tell Mrs McKetchnie as well.'

'Are you sure you don't want us to come with you?' asked Holly.

Bobby shook his head. 'I'd rather do it by myself.' He gave them a wan smile. 'I'm sorry I lied to you,' he said. 'I'm really sorry about the whole thing. And the worst of it is that there'll be no money to help protect the birds now. I've made a complete mess of it.'

Holly put her hand on his arm. 'Good luck,' she said. 'I'm sure the police will understand.'

The three girls watched as Bobby headed down the road to Glenroch.

'I hope they do believe him,' Belinda said uncertainly. 'I'm not sure I would in their position.'

They opened the cottage door and were met by the cheerfully barking Rosie.

'Good heavens,' said Christina, coming out of the dining-room. 'I was beginning to wonder where

97

you'd got to.' She smiled. 'Another couple of hours and I'd have called out the search parties for you. You look tired out.'

'We are,' sighed Holly. 'It's been quite a day!'

They spent the evening in the cottage, recovering from their long walk. They told Christina about seeing the osprey, and about their trip to the far side of the loch – although they avoided any mention of Bobby and the money.

'She'll find out soon enough,' Holly whispered to the others when Christina went through to the kitchen to prepare dinner.

'Can we help you?' Tracy called from the dining-room door.

'You can lay the table for me,' Christina called back. 'All the things are in the cabinet.'

'Ask her about that bird sanctuary thing,' said Belinda as they spread a fresh cloth on the long, polished oak table. 'I want to make sure Bobby was telling us the truth.'

'Don't you trust him?' asked Tracy.

'Do you blame me?' said Belinda. 'He hasn't exactly been honest with us up to now.'

'How are the preparations for the concert going?' Holly asked Christina, once dinner had been brought through.

'I've got my fingers crossed,' said Christina. 'But

I think it'll be OK. We've got the musicians lined up. All we need now is plenty of people to come along.'

'We'll come,' said Belinda. 'What charity is it for?'

'We're trying to raise money to buy a plot of land and turn it into a bird sanctuary,' said Christina.

'Oh, good!' said Tracy. Holly gave her a warning look. She didn't want Tracy blurting out the whole story.

'I – I mean it's good that the birds should have somewhere safe,' stammered Tracy, noticing Holly's eyes on her.

Holly was relieved as well. At least now they knew that Bobby's story was true.

They watched television for a while after dinner, but it wasn't long before Belinda was nodding in her chair.

'It's no good,' she said. 'If I don't go to bed, I'm going to crash out right here.' She stifled a yawn. 'I'll see you in the morning.'

'I think I'll go up as well,' said Tracy. 'I want to do a few exercises before I go to bed.'

Belinda stared at her. 'You're mad,' she said. 'Haven't you had enough exercise for one day?'

'I always do a few exercises last thing,' said Tracy, looking at Belinda. 'You should try it; it really helps you relax before sleeping.'

'I don't need to relax to sleep,' said Belinda. 'I just need a bed.'

The two girls went upstairs. Holly didn't like to move just then. Rosie was asleep across her feet, and it seemed a shame to disturb her.

'You look tired as well,' Christina said after a few minutes.

'I am,' said Holly. 'I was going to watch the end of this programme, but I don't think I'll bother now.' She slid her feet out from under the dog and stretched. Rosie made a few whiffly, snorting noises but didn't wake up.

'It's a long way all round the loch,' said Holly. 'How does Mr Fox cope with being so far from everything?'

'You've heard about Gregory, have you?' said Christina. 'He's our local eccentric. I know him quite well, actually. He's been living over in Iron Stone Croft now for as long as I can remember. He's a retired doctor. He came here for the solitude. He hates people, I can tell you that much, although he's friendly enough to me when I see him.' She smiled. 'I think I'd go a little bit mad up there all on my own. You know, he doesn't even have a radio. The only time he ever gets any news is when he brings his car down to Glenroch for provisions.'

'He's retired, is he?' asked Holly, suddenly alert. 'He's quite old, then?'

'He's in his late sixties, at least,' said Christina.

She laughed. 'Him and his long grey beard. We call him the Old Man of the Mountains. But he's as fit as a fiddle. He could walk me off my feet!' Christina got up and switched the television off. 'I think I'll be off to bed as well,' she said. 'I've got a long day tomorrow. I've got plenty to do if I'm going to take that day off with you.'

But Holly was hardly listening. Her mind was racing back to the brief description she had given Bobby of the fisherman they had seen.

She had mentioned the grey beard, but Bobby had said it *couldn't* be Gregory Fox because he was a younger man. Bobby had lied! But why? Why would Bobby lie about that?

Holly knocked lightly on Belinda's door.

'Belinda? Are you awake?' she whispered, opening the door a little and looking into the darkened room. 'Belinda?'

But there was no sound from the bed other than Belinda's gentle snoring. Downstairs, she heard the sounds of Christina switching off lights and closing doors for the night.

Holly crept along to Tracy's room. At least Tracy's light was still on.

'Tracy?' she called softly.

'What?'

Holly slid quietly into the room and closed the door behind herself. Tracy was sitting up in bed with a tourist brochure across her knees.

'I've got to talk to you,' said Holly. 'I've just found out something about Gregory Fox.'

'Who?' said Tracy.

'The man who lives at Iron Stone Croft,' said Holly.

'Oh, right, the hermit,' said Tracy. 'What about him?'

Holly sat on the edge of Tracy's bed and told her what Christina McKetchnie had just said.

'But why would Bobby lie to us?' said Tracy.

'I don't know,' said Holly. 'That's why I wanted to talk about it. What's Bobby up to? He must have known perfectly well that it was Mr Fox that we saw. So why pretend it wasn't?' She frowned. 'I think Bobby's still playing games with us.'

'Do you think he told us a pack of lies back there?' said Tracy. 'About wanting the money for the bird sanctuary?'

'I don't know what to think now,' said Holly. 'But I'll tell you one thing – he's not going to get away with it, whatever he's doing. I don't like someone trying to make a fool of me.' She gave Tracy a determined look. 'We're going to get to the bottom of this,' she said. 'Even if it means going to the police ourselves!'

8 Missing!

The bedroom was quite dark when Holly woke up the next morning. She leaned out of bed and pulled the curtain open, thinking that maybe she'd woken up earlier than normal. Up until then, she had woken to see the light shining brightly through the curtains.

The overnight change in the weather was dramatic. The cold westerly breeze of the previous evening had pulled in a dense blanket of low-lying cloud. The loch water gleamed under the heavy cloud like dull metal. The mountains were grey, their tops blurry and indistinct.

Holly got dressed and met up with Tracy in the hallway.

'What happened to the summer?' said Tracy. 'Have you seen those clouds?'

They went to rouse Belinda and to tell her about Gregory Fox. Belinda sat on the edge of her bed, thoughtfully polishing her spectacles.

'What's that boy up to now?' she said.

'Maybe he just got it wrong?' suggested Tracy.

Her forehead wrinkled as she saw the disbelieving looks that Holly and Belinda gave her. She shook her head. 'No,' she said. 'I guess he couldn't have got it wrong. But why would he lie about something as stupid as that? If he knew it was Mr Fox who had found the case, why didn't he just say so?'

'Because he's up to something,' said Belinda. 'And I'll tell you something else. I'll bet you anything you like that he didn't go to the police.'

'Do you think we should tell Christina about it all?' asked Tracy.

'I think we should,' said Belinda.

'Not yet,' said Holly. 'Let's go to the hotel first. If we find out that Bobby hasn't been to the police, we'll let him know that we're not prepared to cover for him any more. We'll tell him that either he goes straight to the police himself, or we'll drag him there.'

Over breakfast the three of them listened intently to the radio. The local news bulletin would surely have something to say about the money being found.

But there was nothing. Nothing except the news that Declan Pallow and the stolen money were still missing and that the police had widened the search area. It was clear from the broadcast that the police still thought Pallow was in possession of the money.

'What have you girls got planned for today,

then?' asked Christina as they collected their breakfast plates from the kitchen.

'Not sunbathing, that's for sure,' said Belinda. 'Do you think it's going to stay like this for very long?'

'I'm afraid it might,' said Christina. 'There are train excursions along the coast, you know. Why don't I drive you into Glenroch? You could get a train from there. Even in this weather, the scenery will be worth looking at – and at least you won't get wet if it rains.'

'We were thinking of going to see Bobby Talisker this morning,' said Holly. 'But we could go for a train ride afterwards.'

'I'll drop you off at the hotel, then,' said Christina. 'But I'd dress up warmly, if I were you. There's a sharp wind today and the forecast said it would probably rain.'

Fortunately all three girls had brought warm coats. They were thankful for them as they waited outside the cottage door. Christina had been right about the wind. It came whipping across the loch, flecking the surface with white and bending the trees in its path.

'It's like autumn,' said Belinda with a shiver, as she climbed into the car. Rosie was frisking round them. As Belinda sat down, Rosie leaped into the car, landing heavily across her lap.

'No, no,' said Christina. 'Not this time, Rosie.

Out you get. You stay here and look after the cottage.'

The dog slid reluctantly out of the car, watching them with envious eyes as they drove away.

'I'm afraid this is what the Scottish summer is like,' said Christina. 'You can't trust the weather from one day to the next.'

Christina dropped the girls off at the road that led to the Angel Hotel.

'I'll be back some time this afternoon,' Christina told them. 'But you can contact me at the pub if you need me for anything. The number's by the phone.' She waved a hand out of the car window as she drove off.

'Bye,' called the girls as the car bumped its way round the curve and disappeared.

'OK, Mr Bobby Talisker,' said Belinda as they headed for the hotel. 'This time we're going to get the truth out of you. No more games!'

A couple of guests were standing in the lobby looking at tourist guides. Holly rang the bell at the reception desk and a middle aged man appeared.

'Would it be possible for us to have a quick word with Bobby Talisker?' Holly asked politely.

The man frowned. 'You're not the only one who wants a word with that young man,' he said. He tapped his wristwatch. 'Half past seven he's supposed to start work. I've told him often enough about time-keeping.'

106

'You mean he isn't here?' asked Belinda.

'He is not,' said the man. 'He must have gone out at the crack of dawn. It'll be those birds again! Chef is tearing his hair out.' The man glared at the three girls. 'Who's going to wash up the breakfast things, that's what I want to know? Ospreys! I'll give that laddie ospreys when I catch him!'

'Sorry to have bothered you,' said Belinda, backing away. 'If we see Bobby, we'll tell him you're looking for him.'

'Aye, do that,' said the man. 'And tell him I'm going to tear his hide off and hang it from a tree!'

The three girls beat a hasty retreat.

'Maybe he's gone to the police this morning?' said Tracy.

'Or maybe he hasn't,' said Belinda. She looked at Holly. 'Well?' she said. 'What do we do now?'

'Try to find him, I suppose,' said Holly. 'There are two places where he might be. Either in the woods where the birds are nesting, or on that headland where he took us yesterday. He told us he goes there a lot, especially in the mornings.'

'And if we don't find him?' said Belinda.

'Then I suppose we'll have to go to the police ourselves,' said Holly. She looked at her friends. 'But let's give him one last chance, eh?'

The woodland was quite different today; full of noise and movement as the wind whipped through the branches. They huddled in their coats, calling

107

Bobby's name. But the fierce wind swept their voices away through the damp gloom that gathered round them.

'We'll get lost again,' warned Belinda after they had spent some time shouting themselves hoarse without even a glimpse of Bobby Talisker. 'If we're not lost already!'

'It's OK,' said Tracy. 'This time, I know exactly where we are. The tree where the ospreys nest is over there.'

They followed Tracy deeper into the woodland.

'Oh!' said Tracy, as they came to the edge of the woods and found themselves looking out over a rough meadow beyond a low wire fence. 'This can't be right.' She looked round at her friends. 'I was sure it was this way. We must have missed it.'

'*We*?' said Belinda. 'We were just following *you*!'

'We're not going to find him in here,' said Holly. 'Look, let's make our way back round the woods. He might be over by the loch.' She climbed the fence and dropped down into the tall meadow grass. 'If we go this way, there's no chance of us getting lost.'

Tracy jumped over the fence and Belinda was just putting one leg over the top when something caught her eye and she stopped.

'I'd get back over here, if I were you,' she said.

'Why?' asked Holly. 'What's wrong?'

'Take a look over there,' said Belinda, pointing

along the fence. A large, shaggy, tan-coloured shape stood close to the fence. Even as Holly and Tracy looked, the animal lifted its head from grazing and they saw the broad, wide sweep of its horns.

'It's only a cow!' said Tracy. 'You're not scared of cows, are you?'

'No,' said Belinda. 'I'm not scared of cows. But that cow isn't a cow. That cow is a bull!'

'Oh, crumbs,' said Holly. 'It must be the one Christina told us about. The *fierce* one.'

'You pair are really scaredy-cats,' said Tracy. 'It's not going to take any notice of us.' She walked away from the fence. 'Hi, bull!' she called. 'You don't mind us walking round your field, do you?' She turned and grinned at Holly and Belinda. 'You see?' she said. 'What did I tell you?'

Belinda looked at the bull. It certainly didn't show any particular sign of being about to charge them. Maybe Tracy was right.

'Are you coming over here, or what?' asked Tracy.

'I'm coming,' Belinda said, as she carefully climbed over the fence. 'Tracy – don't go over there, you idiot. You'll annoy it!'

'Aw, poo!' said Tracy, walking towards the placid-looking creature. 'It's about as dangerous as a – oops!'

Tracy was only a few metres away from the

bull when it suddenly snorted and stamped a hoof.

'Tracy!' yelled Belinda. 'Get back here, you idiot. It's coming!'

The huge bull lumbered into movement. Tracy's eyes widened as the shaggy creature picked up speed and came thundering through the grass towards her.

Belinda was back over the fence in a split second, Holly only moments behind her as the bull hurtled towards them.

Tracy sprinted alongside the fence, only a metre or so ahead of the charging bull.

Holly and Belinda yelled encouragement as Tracy made a sudden swerve out into the field and the bull went thundering past her.

The two girls jumped back as Tracy pulled round in a tight circle through the grass and came racing towards the fence.

'Quickly!' yelled Holly. The bull had turned and was charging back along the fence.

Tracy flung herself into the air. She was halfway over the fence when her jacket snagged on a piece of wire. She struggled, wrenching frantically at it.

Belinda sprang forwards and grabbed Tracy by the collar, tipping her forwards over the fence. Only just in time! As she was up-ended over the fence, Tracy felt the edge of the bull's horn graze across her leg.

110

Tracy scrambled to her feet and the three of them backed into the trees as the bull pounded to a halt and stared aggressively at them over the flimsy wire. It gave a snort and stamped, lowering its huge head as though it meant to charge right through the fence to get at them.

'It's OK.' Belinda shouted at the bull. 'You win! We'll find another way round.'

'Dumb bull!' said Tracy. 'We weren't doing anything!'

'I don't think he's listening,' said Holly. 'Let's get out of here.'

'Huh!' said Tracy. 'He doesn't scare me.'

The bull snorted and butted its horns against the fence.

'Oh, heck,' gasped Tracy as the fence rattled alarmingly. 'I don't know, though!'

The three girls turned and ran back into the trees.

'Well?' asked Belinda, as the three of them stood on the deserted headland in the full force of the wind. 'He's not here. Do we talk to the police now?'

Holly nodded, her hair whipping in her face. They had done their best to try and find Bobby. They really had no other option now than to head down to Glenroch and tell the police everything they knew. Even Bobby would understand that they couldn't keep a secret like that for any longer.

'It's kind of strange, though,' said Tracy as they

111

walked along the earth road. 'How come there was nothing on the radio this morning about the money being found? That Fox guy had plenty of time to hand it in yesterday, but the newscaster said it was still missing.'

'Maybe the police haven't told anyone yet,' said Holly.

'Or maybe Mr Fox saw all that money and decided to keep it for himself,' said Tracy.

'No, wait!' said Holly. 'Bobby said he unlocked the case with a key, right? But if he locked the case again and *took* the key, Mr Fox won't have been able to open it, not unless he was prepared to break it open. He might not even know there was any money in it.'

'He can't be that thick,' said Belinda. 'Even a total idiot would be able to put two and two together and figure out that the case was the one everyone was searching for.'

'Only if he *knew* about the stolen money,' Holly said excitedly. 'I was chatting to Christina last night. She said he's a total recluse. She said he doesn't even have a radio. And she said he only goes into town now and then for food and stuff.' She looked eagerly at her friends. 'What if he hasn't been into town in the past few days? He might know nothing about it.'

'He'll know about the plane crash,' said Belinda. 'He can't have missed *that*.'

'No, but if he doesn't have a radio, he won't know about the stolen money,' said Holly. 'He might think the case had been lost off a boat, or something.'

'But even a complete hermit would realise someone has lost it,' said Tracy. 'He wouldn't just keep it.'

'Of course not,' said Holly. 'But if he doesn't know how important it is, he might have decided he'd take it into town next time he goes there, rather than make a special trip. Christina said he hates meeting people. For all we know, he's still got the case!'

'Maybe that's what Bobby was counting on!' exclaimed Belinda. 'And that's why he didn't want us to know that Mr Fox found the case! He must be hoping to get it back before Mr Fox takes it into town.'

'But Bobby couldn't go over there yesterday because we were with him,' said Holly. She stared over towards the misty hills across the loch. 'And that's where he is now! That's where he's gone!'

But even if Holly's theory was right, that didn't help the girls to decide what they should do next. Belinda was still convinced that they should go to the police.

'What else can we do?' she said. 'We can't keep covering up for Bobby. We'll end up in trouble ourselves. We're not talking about a few pounds,

113

here. There's fifty *thousand* pounds missing. And we know something about it. We've got to go to the police.'

'You're right,' said Holly. 'We gave Bobby his chance yesterday. Are we all agreed?'

'Agreed,' said Tracy. 'I wish we'd never found out about any of this. I wish Declan Pallow *had* run off with the money, like everyone else thinks. I hate to think how much trouble this is going to get Bobby into.' She looked unhappily at her two friends. 'And he was only doing it for the birds.'

'That's no excuse,' said Belinda. 'That's like saying stealing is OK if it's for a good cause. I expect Pallow thought he had a good reason for stealing it in the first place.'

'Well, Pallow hasn't got the money now,' said Holly. 'That's something.' The wind gusted round them and a flurry of fine, chilling rain prickled on their skin.

'It's going to pour down,' said Belinda with a shiver. 'We'll get soaked. What say we just go back to Christina's and phone the police from there? There's nothing we could tell them in person that we can't say over the phone.'

By the time they neared the cottage, the rain was slanting down through the grey sky with a keen, cutting edge. The clouds seemed to have come in even lower, shrouding the mountains so that they looked almost ghostly in the failing light.

'Poor Rosie,' said Tracy. 'I hope she's found somewhere dry to hide out.'

With their eyes screwed tight against the rain, the girls ran for the cottage, their feet sending up splashes of mud as they made for the door.

'Hello,' said Belinda. 'A car!'

It was an old, orange estate car, facing away from them with the driver's door flung wide open. The car was standing alone on the road some fifty metres away from the cottage.

They approached it. Why had someone abandoned the car like that, leaving the door open?

'Weird,' said Tracy. She looked towards the cottage. 'Hey, look!' she shouted. 'The front door is open.'

'Burglars!' said Belinda.

'Do they have burglars up here?' said Tracy.

'I don't know,' said Belinda. 'If it's not burglars, maybe whoever owns the car has gone to the cottage for shelter.'

'But how would they get the door open?' exclaimed Holly. 'It was locked!' Holly gripped Tracy's arm. 'Look!' she gasped. 'There!'

A figure was moving through the reeds that grew on the bank above the beach. It was huddled in a dark blue anorak with the hood up against the rain. Holly had seen that anorak before. Two days ago. She was certain of it. It had the same orange stripe across the shoulders. It was the same one

115

that had been worn by that elusive figure in the trees.

'It's Pallow!' she breathed. 'I know it is!'

'He wouldn't have a car,' said Belinda.

'He could have stolen it,' said Holly. 'And look, he's heading for Christina's boat! Come on, we've got to try and stop him! He must have broken into the cottage and stolen the keys. It's definitely the man I saw in the woods! We mustn't let him get away!'

It was obvious to the other two that Holly was right about one thing. The running man was making for the jetty where Christina's motorboat was moored.

'Come on!' said Tracy. 'We can't just stand here watching him!'

They raced through the rain, their feet skidding on the slippery mud as they pelted down to the beach.

The man was already by the boat. They saw him untie the mooring rope and climb aboard.

'Stop!' shouted Tracy. 'Hey! Stop!' But the wind that blasted into her face deadened her voice.

They ran along the jetty, all three of them shouting now.

The boat's motor roared against the howl of the wind. But at last the man had heard them. He gave a start and stared round at them. The hood of his anorak was pulled up tight around his face. All they could see were his nose and a pair of startled eyes.

Tracy jumped on to the boat and it rocked alarmingly, sending her sliding off-balance across the rain-wet deck.

Holly saw Tracy fall, and saw the man's arms windmill as he fought for balance. Holly was on the boat in a second, determined that Tracy shouldn't have to face the man on her own.

Belinda was only half a pace behind her, but before she could do anything, the boat was already moving away from the jetty.

'Holly!' she screamed as half a metre of choppy grey water opened up under her feet. She lurched forwards, desperately trying to catch hold of the edge of the boat and somehow stop it from moving away. But she wasn't strong enough to fight the motor.

For a split second she hung, her feet trailing on the jetty and her arms clinging to the side of the boat.

Belinda's additional weight brought the side of the boat down and the deck tilted like the roof of a house. It was impossible for Holly to keep to her feet, and as she tumbled over she saw the man's arms flailing as he fell with a muffled shout over the side.

There was a tremendous splash as the boat tipped to and fro. Holly saw Belinda's frightened face as

117

she clung to the side of the boat. And as if all that wasn't bad enough, the boat was moving out into the loch, its motor growling above the noise of the rainstorm.

Holly saw Belinda's hands slip and saw the look of panic on her friend's face. Another second and Belinda would lose her grip and plunge into the choppy waters of the loch.

9 Innis Maer

Belinda felt her legs dragged away through the icy water as the motorboat slewed away from the jetty. It was rocking less wildly now and she was able to get an elbow up over the side. But the woodwork was slippery from the rain. She felt her hold failing, her fingers sliding as she scrabbled her feet against the boat's hull.

Holly slithered across the deck and managed to grab hold of Belinda's wrists.

'Tracy! Help!' she cried.

Tracy had fallen heavily, jarring her shoulder, and bumping her head. But she ignored the pain as she crawled across the deck and helped Holly drag Belinda aboard.

'It's OK!' she gasped, as Belinda came rolling over the side of the boat. 'We've got you!'

'What about Pallow?' panted Belinda.

The motorboat was already several metres away from the jetty, leaving a white wake of churned-up water. Holly dashed the teeming rain out of her eyes.

The man was safe! He had swum to the jetty and was working his way along towards the shore.

Now that the mad rocking of the boat had stopped, the girls were able to get to their feet.

'Grab the wheel,' shouted Belinda.

Tracy was nearest to the steering-wheel. She pounced forwards and locked her hands round it.

'What do I do?' she shouted. The motorboat had already cut its way far out into the loch, ploughing at full speed through the churning water.

'Turn it,' said Belinda.

Tracy hauled at the steering-wheel. 'It won't!' she cried. 'It won't turn!'

'Of course it will,' said Belinda, catching hold of her friend to steady herself.

'It *won't*!' wailed Tracy, struggling vainly to move the wheel.

'There must be some kind of locking mechanism,' said Belinda. 'A lever or something.'

In a wild panic, Tracy grabbed at the key that hung from the ignition. She didn't have the faintest idea how the boat worked, but she twisted the key, in the hope that something would happen.

The motor died suddenly, as Tracy pulled the key out.

'You twit!' said Belinda. 'You've turned it off!'

'Well, that's better than just keeping going, surely?' said Tracy.

'No, it isn't,' said Belinda, giving Tracy a push

to one side as she took hold of the steering-wheel. 'We can't steer this thing without the motor! Give me the key!'

But as she reached out, her elbow banged against Tracy's arm, making Tracy slip on the wet boards.

Instinctively, Tracy snatched at the metal rail that ran across the front of the cabin. The key flew out of her hand, sliding along the sloping cabin roof.

'No!' shrieked Belinda as the key skidded along the polished wooden surface. She hurled herself forwards, snatching for the key. But she was too late. Her hand came slapping down a centimetre away from the key as it slid over the side of the boat.

With a yell, Tracy hung over the side, as if she expected the key to be floating on the water. But there wasn't even a ripple to show where it had plummeted into the loch.

'Look what you've done!' shouted Belinda.

'It wasn't my fault,' said Tracy. 'You knocked into me!'

Belinda banged her hands down on the unmoving steering-wheel.

'This is just perfect!' she said. 'Now what on earth do we do?'

'Maybe there are some paddles?' said Tracy.

'Of course there aren't any paddles,' snapped Belinda. 'This is a motorboat. You use the motor!

At least, you do if some prize idiot hasn't slung the key overboard!'

'It can't be helped now,' said Holly. 'Belinda, you know more about boats than we do. Is there any way of getting us back to land?'

'Not unless Tracy fancies swimming back with the tow rope between her teeth,' said Belinda.

Holly looked back to the receding shoreline. The man in the blue anorak was out of the water now, sitting in the seaweed with his head in his hands.

'I'm not taking all the blame for this,' said Tracy. 'Why didn't one of you grab the rope while we were still by the jetty?'

'Why didn't *you*?' said Belinda. 'I was too busy trying not to fall in the water.'

The boat had slowed down now, but it was a long way from the shore. The surface of the loch was jumping from the rain that beat steadily down on them.

'This is hopeless,' said Holly. 'He's going to get away! Isn't there anything we can do?'

'Even if we could move this darned wheel,' said Belinda, 'we can't steer without the motor running.'

'Could we jump-start it?' asked Tracy. 'You know, like people do with cars?'

'Do you know how to do that?' asked Belinda. 'Because I certainly don't.'

'Oh, heck!' groaned Tracy. 'This is all my fault! I'm so dumb!'

'It's not all your fault,' said Belinda. 'I suppose you can't help being clumsy.' She wiped her fingers across her spectacles. 'I can hardly see a thing,' she said. She looked at Holly. 'What are we going to do?'

'What can we do?' asked Holly.

'Flares!' exclaimed Belinda. 'Boats always carry flares in case of trouble.'

'Of course! If we set off a flare, we'll be rescued in no time,' said Holly. But the glimmer of hope soon faded; their frantic search turned up nothing even resembling a flare.

'Oh well, we're bound to drift ashore eventually,' said Belinda. It was clear that the tide was taking them further away from the shores of Angel Bay, and further down the loch.

'Unless we end up out at sea,' said Tracy.

The other two looked at her.

'Well, thanks for sharing *that* thought with us,' said Belinda. 'That's cheered me up no end!'

'We might hit land down near Glenroch,' Holly said hopefully. 'If that happens, we'll be able to get to the police station and tell them we've found Pallow.'

'If it is Pallow,' said Tracy.

'It must be,' said Holly. 'Who else would try to steal Christina's boat?'

123

'But why would he want the boat?' asked Tracy. 'He had a car. And where would he have got a car from in the first place?'

'He must have stolen it,' said Holly. 'And how should I know why he wanted the boat? Perhaps he thought the roads would all be watched. Perhaps he meant to take the boat right down the coast.'

'He's heading back to the car,' said Belinda, peering through the rain. The distant figure was heading up the beach.

'He's going to get away,' Holly said forlornly. 'And we're going to have to just *sit* here!' She peered along the coast. 'Unless someone spots us and we can signal for help.'

'That could take forever,' said Belinda. 'The way the tide's taking us, if we don't think of *something*, we might *really* end up at sea.'

They could all see their peril. The shores of Loch Evayne were a hundred metres or more away now, and getting further and further away as the tide drew the stranded boat out into the middle of the loch.

The only tiny piece of comfort was that the wind had died down and the rain was falling less heavily.

'We could try swimming,' said Tracy.

'I can't swim that far,' said Belinda.

'What about trying to get to the island?' said Holly. The dark hump of Innis Maer rose out of the loch a few hundred metres away. As the girls followed the line of Holly's eyes, they could see that the boat was creeping steadily towards the island on the tide.

But there was something in the water, between the boat and the island. At first, the girls thought they were bubbles – large, whitish bubbles floating on the surface. But they were too big – about the size of dinner plates. Three or four of them were lying in the water.

'Jellyfish,' said Belinda with a shiver.

'They might not be the really nasty ones,' said Holly.

'I don't care if they're the cutest jellyfish in the world,' said Belinda. 'All jellyfish sting! I'm staying on this boat!'

The boat turned slowly, edging closer to the island. There was a low grating sound and the boat shuddered, its stern turning.

'There must be rocks under the surface,' said Holly, as the grating sound echoed through the hull. They leaned over the side. Beneath the moving, rain-pocked skin of the loch, they could see grim, dark shapes.

'That's all we need,' said Belinda. 'A big hole ripped out of the bottom!'

The boat turned round slowly, jarring as it hit against another rock. Ahead of them the rocks that surrounded Innis Maer lifted slimy, seaweedy

125

heads, the dark green trailers of seaweed streaming in the flow of water.

Now that the island was so close, they could see that it wasn't as barren as they had thought. Above the girdle of seaweed, the steep ridges were covered in spiny bushes and grasses, a hard growth of plant-life that clung fast to the island's rugged hide.

Only a few metres of water, swirling round the rocks, separated them from the island now.

The boat came to a juddering halt, caught between two shoulders of rock.

The girls looked at one another.

'I think we'd be safer on the island,' said Holly.

Belinda looked at the slimy knuckles of rock that held the boat.

'OK,' she said. 'Let's go for it. We're more likely to be seen up there, anyway.'

One by one, the girls climbed over the side of the boat. The rocks gave perilous footholds, and the weed was very slippery. They held hands, Holly in the lead, picking their way with painful caution along the shoulders of rock towards the main bulk of the island.

Holly jumped the final narrow channel on to a slithery angle of land between two rearing columns of rock. She held out her hands for Belinda and soon all three of them were safely on the island.

Tracy looked back at the boat. It was being

held tightly between two jaws of rock. The slow tide moved round it, but it didn't move. It was locked solid.

It only took half a minute for them to climb up to the highest point on the island. Innis Maer was a rugged oval of rock and shrubs, pitted with deep clefts. The entire island couldn't have been more than a hundred metres long.

Belinda shivered, wrapping her arms round herself for warmth.

'How long before someone finds us?' she said.

Holly looked at her watch. It wasn't even noon. They could be stranded there for hours before Christina came home and discovered that the boat was missing.

'Someone is bound to see us,' she said. 'All we've got to do is sit tight and wait.'

'Sit?' said Belinda. 'We can't even do that. It's too wet to sit down. Everything's wet!' She crouched down, huddled into a miserable bundle. 'And while we're stuck here, Declan Pallow is getting away!' She looked up at Tracy. 'This has got to be the worst day of my entire life!'

'I'm sorry,' said Tracy. 'I didn't drop that key on purpose. I'm just as sick about this as you are. Oh, Lord! I wish we could *do* something.'

'Why don't you?' said Belinda. 'All you've got to do is swim over to the cottage and call the police.'

127

Tracy gave her a hurt look.

'OK,' she said. 'I know it's my fault we're stuck here.'

'Too right, it is!' snapped Belinda.

Holly looked anxiously at her two friends. 'At least the rain is easing off,' she said. 'And the clouds are breaking up a bit over there.' Away down the loch a glimmer of washed-out blue sky showed through the cloud banks.

'Great,' said Belinda. 'We'll be able to sunbathe!'

Tracy gave her friend an unhappy look and wandered away, her arms round herself for warmth. She came to the far edge of the flattened summit of the island. Rocks tumbled down to a narrow, seaweedy strip of land. Her eyes widened and she let out a gasp.

'Holly! Belinda! Look!' Tracy could hardly believe her eyes. A small rowing-boat was drawn up out of the water. Tracy gave a yell of joy. 'There's a boat!'

The others ran to join her, all their misery forgotten as they stared down at the boat. A pair of oars lay across the seating planks.

'Saved!' yelled Belinda. 'I don't believe it! Let's get down there!'

'But what's it doing here?' said Holly. 'It can't have got here on its own.'

'Who cares?' said Tracy. 'It's here!' She cast round

for a safe way down to the boat. 'We can row across to the cottage!'

'Warmth!' whooped Belinda. 'And dry clothes! And then we can phone the police.'

'That's right,' said Tracy. 'Declan Pallow isn't going to get away after all!'

Holly was as delighted as the others at the discovery of the boat, but as she followed them round to the place where Tracy was already scrambling down to the small beach, she couldn't help wondering how the boat had got there.

It was above the seaweed line, so it couldn't simply have drifted ashore. Someone had dragged it clear of the water. Which meant he must still be on the island. But if that was the case, why hadn't he shown himself? Whoever it was, he must have heard the girls' voices. He must know the three of them were stranded there.

'Tracy, wait,' called Holly. 'There's something strange about this.'

But Tracy wasn't listening. She skidded down the stony slope on her backside with Belinda close behind.

'Wheee-hah!' whooped Belinda as her feet crunched into the shingle. 'The Mystery Club rides again! Come on, Holly! What are you waiting for? A written invitation?'

Holly shook her head and made her way down the slope to her friends.

Tracy was already at the boat, hanging on to the prow and trying to drag it round through the shingle.

'Anyone know how to row?' she shouted.

'I do,' said Belinda, helping Tracy to turn the boat.

Holly ran across the shingle.

'Someone must have brought the boat over here,' she said.

'It was probably our guardian angel,' said Belinda with a laugh. 'Saint Tracy – the patron saint of dozy people!'

'Hey! Do you mind!' said Tracy.

'Nope,' laughed Belinda. 'I don't mind at all. Not now Saint Tracy has sent us a boat to get us out of here.'

'But who brought this boat over here?' insisted Holly. 'Someone must have rowed it to the island. But where are they now? Don't you see? Where could they have gone?'

Belinda stared at her. As the excitement of their discovery ebbed away, she realised the truth of what Holly was saying.

'*Two* boats?' she said uncertainly. 'Or . . . or maybe they swam back?'

'That's just silly!' said Holly.

'Are you two going to have a debate about this?' demanded Tracy. 'Or are we going to get off this island?'

'You're going to do nothing!' said a strange voice.

The girls spun round. There was a cleft in the sheer wall of rock – a narrow cave-like depression under the beetling brow of the cliff. And at the mouth of this cave, a man stood watching them with sunken, hooded eyes.

He was wearing a stained and rumpled jacket and his clothes were dirty and creased. His face was sallow and unshaven, his grey hair tangled. But what sent Holly's heart hammering up into her throat was the livid wound on the man's forehead. It was caked with dried blood, and there were more traces of blood on his face and on the front of his jacket.

He took a step forwards, thrusting his hand into the pocket of his jacket and lifting it so that it was pointed towards the girls.

He took another shaky step. Holly thought that he looked on the point of exhaustion, but there was a deadly light in his red-rimmed eyes.

'I've got a gun,' he said. 'You will do exactly what I tell you. And if you don't . . .' He paused, thrusting the hidden weapon towards them. 'I will kill you.'

10 Tracy says too much

'Pallow!' breathed Holly as the haggard man stood, swaying slightly in front of them. She couldn't believe how stupid she had been. From the very first sight of the rowing-boat she had known there was something wrong. She had sensed from the first moment that they should be careful.

An abandoned boat, only a narrow stretch of water away from the place where the aeroplane had come down. A missing man and a lonely island. How many more clues did she need, for heaven's sake?

If only she'd thought for a second. But she'd been too eager to get off the island to put two and two together. And now the three of them were trapped.

And the sudden appearance of Pallow sent another thought tumbling through Holly's mind. Who was the man they had encountered back at the cottage? The man who had fallen off the motorboat. Who was *he*?

Pallow stumbled towards them, the hidden gun

thrusting menacingly from the point of his mud-caked jacket.

'I need food,' he said, his bloodshot eyes desperate. 'Have you got any food with you?'

'N – no,' stammered Tracy.

'I have,' said Belinda. She pulled a packet of oatcakes out of her pocket. Her previous trips out had taught her to bring at least *some* food along with her, and she had taken the packet of biscuits from the cupboard before they had started out. 'Here – take them.'

Pallow snatched the small packet out of her hand, backing away as he tore the plastic film off with his teeth and crammed a biscuit into his mouth.

He ate ravenously, his eyes constantly on the three girls. Holly glanced up towards the left where he had been hiding. She could see a small bag and something that looked like a transistor radio. Lying by the bag was a large empty plastic water bottle. So Pallow had sustained himself with bottled water while he had been in hiding. But from the way he devoured the thin oatcakes, he probably hadn't eaten for days. No wonder he looked so shaky on his legs.

Pallow wiped his hand across his mouth.

'What else have you got?' he croaked. 'You must have more food than this.'

'We haven't,' said Belinda. 'But there's plenty of food at the cottage.' She waved vaguely in the direction of Angel Bay, hidden now behind the rearing spine of Innis Maer. 'All you have to do is row over there,' she said.

'What cottage?' said Pallow.

'Bay View Cottage,' said Belinda. 'You'll be safe. There's no one there.'

Pallow's eyes narrowed and he nodded slowly. 'I've seen it,' he said. 'And I've seen the lights at night over there. Is there a car?'

'Yes, but – 'began Tracy, but Belinda interrupted her.

'Yes!' she said. 'The car's there! And the cottage isn't locked. All you'd have to do is row over there and you could use the car to get away. We wouldn't stop you.'

A wolfish grin passed over Pallow's face. 'You wouldn't stop me?' he snarled. 'That's good of you.'

'I – I mean, we couldn't stop you,' said Belinda.

Pallow nodded. 'That's true,' he said. He looked at Tracy. 'What were you going to say?'

'Nothing,' said Tracy. 'I was just going to say the same as Belinda.'

'Do you think I'm stupid?' he said. 'If the car's there, there must be someone in the cottage. Do you think I'm just going to row over there and let myself be seen?'

'It's OK,' said Holly. 'There isn't anyone at the cottage. That's the truth.'

135

'We're not lying to you,' said Tracy. 'Christina has driven into town. She'll be there all day.'

'If she's driven into town, how can the car still be there?' snarled Pallow. He glared at Belinda. 'One more lie out of you!' He waved the hidden gun, his meaning very clear. 'Is there a car there?'

'No,' said Belinda.

'Are the police still searching the area?' said Pallow.

'What police?' asked Holly.

'Don't pretend you don't know what's going on,' said Pallow. 'You know who I am – which means you know all the rest.' He stared at Tracy. 'You said you were going to row over to the cottage and phone the police. You said, "Declan Pallow isn't going to get away after all." Now! Be quick about it – have the police given up searching round here?'

'You know as much as we do,' said Holly. She nodded towards the cleft in the cliff-face. 'You've got a radio. You must have heard the news bulletins.'

'The batteries ran out yesterday,' said Pallow. 'I'll give you one more chance.' He aimed the hidden gun at Holly, nodding towards the mainland. 'Are the police still over there looking for me?'

'The latest we've heard is that they were widening their search,' said Holly. 'That's all we know.'

'Good,' said Pallow. He rubbed his chin with a grimy hand. 'I need food and water,' he said, his mouth spreading in a grim smile. 'And some hostages might help me get through any road blocks.' He swayed again, as though the weakness was coming over him in waves.

If only he didn't have a gun, thought Holly. Pallow must have lost blood from the cut – and he hadn't eaten for days. If he wasn't armed the Mystery Club would probably be able to overpower him.

'Get the boat into the water,' said Pallow. 'I'm getting off this lump of rock, and you're coming with me.'

There was little point in arguing with him – not while he was holding a gun in front of them.

The three girls shoved the boat down to the water.

'Get in,' said Pallow, following them down to the shore.

'There isn't room for all of us,' said Belinda.

'We'll see about that,' said Pallow. 'Two hostages are as good as three. Who wants to stay here – with a *bullet* in her?'

The three girls climbed into the rocking boat, Tracy and Holly cramming themselves together in the prow.

'You!' said Pallow, looking at Belinda. 'You said you could row. Get the oars, and be quick about it.'

Belinda fitted the oars in the rowlocks as Pallow gave the boat a kick to get it free of the shingle. He climbed awkwardly aboard, one hand still on the gun in his jacket pocket as he sat in the stern.

'Row!' he said.

'Where are we going?' said Belinda.

'Over there,' said Pallow, pointing to the nearby shore – the wooded shore directly opposite Angel Bay.

Belinda rowed, her brain racing as she tried to think of a way out of their predicament.

I know what I'd like to do, she thought. *I'd like to give him a swift smack round the ear with one of these oars*! But it wasn't a desire she could put into action. The oars were heavy. By the time she could have lifted an oar out of its rowlock and swung it at him, Declan Pallow could have shot her.

Save for the splash of the oars and the gasp of Belinda's breath, the journey across the loch was silent. Belinda glanced over her shoulder. The shore was approaching. She caught Holly's eye and saw a familiar look. It was the look that meant Holly had a plan.

The boat's prow scraped into the sand, tilting to one side as it came to a halt. Holly and Tracy jumped out as Belinda shipped the oars. Pallow stood up.

Although she had been expecting something, Belinda was taken by surprise by a piercing shriek from Holly.

'Jellyfish!' screamed Holly, giving the boat a hefty kick. 'Watch out!'

Tracy was quick on the uptake. She pointed at the water behind Pallow and let out a deafening scream.

Pallow's head spun round and he staggered as the boat tilted under his feet.

'Belinda! Run!' yelled Holly. But Belinda was still tangled up with the oars. She gave a yelp as Pallow, unbalanced, came crashing down on top of her, pushing her backwards off the plank seat.

'Stop!' shouted Pallow, pinning Belinda down with one hand. 'Stop or I'll kill her!'

It was over. Even if Holly and Tracy *could* escape before Pallow had recovered enough to stop them, there was no way they were going to leave Belinda behind.

Pallow lumbered to his feet, his red-rimmed eyes blazing.

'One more trick like that,' he said, 'and someone's going to pay for it!'

Miserably, Belinda pulled herself out of the boat. She gave Holly an apologetic look. If only she had been a bit quicker, they might have got away. But it was too late now. They stood in the seaweed, once again held fast by the menace of Declan Pallow's gun.

'Walk!' said Pallow.

They walked up the beach towards the trees.

'You've got this all wrong, you know,' said Holly, trying to keep her voice steady. 'You're going to have to walk for hours before you get anywhere where you'll be able to find a car.'

'That's for sure,' said Tracy. 'You're going to have to take us right round the loch. There are no houses round here except Iron Stone Croft, and—'

'Tracy!' gasped Holly.

'Ha!' croaked Pallow. 'So there is a house near here! Where is it?'

Tracy didn't say anything. She felt terrible. *Me and my big mouth*! she thought. She didn't need to look at Holly to realise what she had done by blurting out about Iron Stone Croft.

'It's up there,' said Holly, pointing up towards the misty hillside. 'But there's nothing there. Just an old man who lives there on his own.'

'But he'll have a car,' said Pallow. 'No one could live up there without some form of transport. And he'll have food.'

The girls scrambled up the steep path through the trees, Pallow only one pace behind them, watching them like a hawk, his gun ready for any sign of escape.

They came up on to the road and into swirling ribbons of freezing mist. The mist curled round the treetops, obscuring the mountains so that it was impossible to say where the mist ended and the low clouds began.

'Which way?' said Pallow, his breath gusting white.

140

'I think it's this way,' said Belinda, pointing to the left.

'You'd better be sure,' said Pallow, motioning with the hand he kept in his pocket.

The road curved away through the trees, making a sharp hairpin turn and rising steeply. The mist was no longer composed of trailing fingers now. As they climbed, it gathered thickly about them until it was all they could do to see the phantom shapes of the trees that lined the road.

And then the ranks of trees ended to one side. Over a low, broken wall, they all saw the spectral sight of Iron Stone Croft. It was similar to Bay View Cottage – a long, low stone building set back from the road. But there the similarity ended. Iron Stone Croft looked dilapidated, its sagging roof green with moss. The upper windows were closed off by planks and other scraps of wood and the ground floor windows looked as if they were quietly rotting away.

There was a low doorway and, to one end, a pair of ruinous old wooden doors, held shut by a rusted iron bar.

The house was in darkness.

Holly felt something hard thrust against her back. Pallow was right behind her, his breath cold on her neck.

'Go and knock,' he said. 'If anyone answers, tell them there's been an accident. Get them to come out here. Tell them someone's been hurt and we need help.' He pushed her forwards roughly.

Holly picked her way towards the door and hammered on the peeling wooden panels.

'Help!' she called, hearing her knocks echoing through the croft. 'Help! Anyone!'

She thought she heard a sound. But it didn't come from beyond the door. If anything, it seemed to come from the end of the cottage – from behind the double doors.

'Hello!' she shouted, knocking again. But there was no further sound. Maybe she had imagined it.

She looked round. 'I don't think there's anyone here,' she said. Pallow moved towards her and listened at the door.

After a moment he crouched and picked up a stone. While Holly was still wondering what he intended to do, Pallow stepped over to a window and smashed the stone against the glass. He put his arm through the hole and jerked the window open.

'Get in and open the door,' he said. Glancing at the anxious faces of her two friends, Holly climbed through the narrow window into a dingy room. She headed straight for the door and came out into a bare hallway.

She opened the door and Pallow pushed Belinda and Tracy into the croft.

'Is there no light in this place?' said Pallow. He found an old fashioned switch. A dim electric light came on. Pallow slammed the door behind them.

Now that there was some light, Holly could see that the croft looked a lot less ruinous on the inside than it seemed from the road. At least it looked habitable. There were carpets on the floor, and the rough stone walls had been given a coat of white paint. Pictures hung on the walls – mostly of seascapes and a few coloured paintings of fish. By the door lay a green canvas bag, and leaning against the angle of the wall was a fishing rod.

Pallow motioned for them to precede him down the hall. They came into a large old-fashioned kitchen and – at last – warmth! The heat was radiating from a huge old cooking range set into an arched fireplace.

Pallow pushed the girls aside and leaned over the range, soaking up the heat that rose from it. There was a large oak table in the middle of the room, showing signs of a recent meal. Pallow pointed to a half-loaf of bread.

'Bring that over here,' he said.

Belinda handed him the loaf and Pallow took a ravenous bite, watching them with his hooded eyes as he chewed, swallowed and tore off another chunk with his teeth.

'See what else there is,' he mumbled through his filled mouth.

143

The girls hunted through the cupboards. There was no fridge, but in a coolbox under the sink they found cheese and butter and some slices of ham.

Pallow pulled a chair over to the range and sat with his back to the black iron, his skin losing its deathly-pale appearance as the warmth seeped into his bones.

'I need something hot,' he said. 'Find me something hot!'

'There might be something in there,' said Holly, pointing to a heavy iron pot on the range. Pallow lifted the lid.

'Stew!' said Pallow. 'Do any of you know how to heat things up on this contraption?'

'I do,' said Belinda. 'We've got an Aga at home – it's the same sort of thing.'

'Do it!' said Pallow. 'And you two – sit there and don't make a move.' He still had his hand in his jacket pocket, not letting them forget that he had a gun.

Belinda stoked the fire and slid the pot on to one of the hot plates.

'What are you going to do?' asked Holly. 'The man who lives here could be back at any time.'

'That's what I'm counting on,' said Pallow. His voice sounded stronger now although his eyes still had that haunted look; the look of someone who has had too little sleep over a long period. 'And when he does, we're driving out of here. And

144

you three are going to help me get past the police.'

'Why don't you just give yourself up?' said Tracy. 'You look like you need a doctor.'

Pallow's hand came up to the wound on his forehead.

'You let me worry about that,' he said.

'At least you ought to bathe it,' said Tracy. 'It looks dirty. You could get an infection. Do you want me to look for some tissues or something?'

'No!' snapped Pallow. 'You stay right where you are.' He looked at Belinda, who was stirring the stew. The smell of warm food drifted through the kitchen. 'Is that ready yet?'

'I think so,' said Belinda.

'Get a bowl,' said Pallow.

Belinda fetched a bowl and a spoon from a cupboard and ladled out some of the thick stew. Pallow snatched the bowl from her and put it in his lap.

Holly watched him. If only for one *second* he'd take his hand out of his pocket, if he would let go of that gun only for a *moment*, they might still be able to rush him. But he ate one-handed, the other hand thrust in his pocket.

'Is it OK?' asked Belinda.

Pallow nodded, spooning the stew into his mouth.

'Can I get some more bowls?' asked Belinda. 'For us?'

'No!' snapped Pallow. 'You get over there with the others and sit down.'

'But we're hungry, too,' said Belinda.

'That's too bad,' said Pallow, glaring at Belinda. 'Get over there!'

Belinda sat at the table with her friends. Pallow ate like a wild animal, cramming the stew into his mouth and swallowing it almost without bothering to chew.

And every mouthful, Holly realised, made him stronger and less easy to overcome. She looked over her shoulder. The mist pressed white against the window.

'You won't get far in this fog,' she said. 'Why don't you just give up? You're never going to find that suitcase with all the money you stole in it.'

'So the police found it?' said Pallow.

'No, they didn't find it – but they'll have it soon,' said Tracy. 'In fact, they've probably got it right now!'

Pallow's eyes narrowed. 'What do you mean by that?' he said.

'She means the police will have found it by now,' Belinda said quickly.

Pallow stared at Tracy. 'No,' he said, 'that's not what she said. She said the police didn't find it.' His eyes gleamed menacingly as he looked at Tracy. 'What do you know about it?'

'I don't know anything,' said Tracy. 'How could I? We only know what we've heard on the radio.'

Pallow dashed the bowl to the floor and sprang towards the table.

'You're lying!' he snarled. For a moment, Tracy thought he was going to wrench her out of her chair, but then he swayed and leaned heavily on the table, his breath laboured. His eyes swam for a moment as he looked dizzily at her. Even warmed by the fire and the stew, he was still weak, but it only took him a few seconds to pull himself together.

He straightened up and pointed the hidden gun at Tracy.

'You will tell me everything,' he said, the blunt thrust of his jacket moving towards Belinda. 'You will tell me everything, if you value her life!'

'No!' cried Holly. 'Don't! We'll tell you. The money was found – but not by the police. There's no point in threatening us. Tracy was telling the truth. So far as we know, it's been taken to the police already.'

'How was it found?' demanded Pallow. 'When?'

'It was found the night you crashed,' said Tracy. 'It was still in the plane.'

Pallow shook his head. 'More lies!' he said. 'Even if it had been found by someone else, they would have given it to the police!' His eyes suddenly widened. 'Ahh!' he said slowly. 'Unless . . . unless the

147

person who found it had no intention of handing it over.' He scratched at his stubbly cheek, trying to make sense of what he was being told. 'No!' This is just more lies! You're trying to fool me. I won't have these lies!'

'Please!' said Holly. 'Calm down. You're frightening us. We're not lying to you. The money was found by a friend of ours – but he didn't realise what it was. Not until yesterday. That's what Tracy meant when she said the police would have it by now. He'll have taken it to them by now.' Holly hoped this garbled version of the truth would convince Pallow. And for all she knew it could be true; at least the part about the police having the money by now. Mr Fox had the case – but Mr Fox wasn't at the croft. The only obvious explanation, so far as Holly could see, was that he had taken the case into Glenroch.

At least, she hoped that was what had happened. The alternative didn't bear thinking about; that Mr Fox still had the case – and that he would turn up at the croft, still in possession of it.

Declan Pallow backed towards the chair and sat down heavily. 'Whether it's true or not,' he said, 'it makes no difference to my plans.' He ran a hand over his sweating forehead. 'You!' he snapped, staring at Belinda. 'Find some aspirin!' His voice lowered. 'I've got to keep my head clear,'

148

he mumbled, almost to himself. 'I've got to get rid of this headache.'

'You need more than aspirin,' said Tracy. 'You need a hospital.' She glanced at Holly. 'You look like you could collapse at any moment.'

Holly knew what that brief glance had meant. *Don't do anything*, Tracy had been warning her. *With any luck, he'll pass out.*

But could they rely on that happening? And what might Pallow do if he felt himself weakening?

'What are you staring at?' snarled Pallow.

'You look ill,' said Holly. 'Why don't you let us help you?'

'I don't need any help,' said Pallow. 'We'll just wait here until the man who lives in this dump gets back.' His eyes became suddenly steely. 'And if anyone makes a move without my say-so, they'll regret it.' The hand with the hidden gun lifted again. 'There are enough bullets to go round,' he said. 'Do I make myself clear?'

'Yes,' said Holly, swallowing a lump in her throat. 'Perfectly clear.'

11   Of ghoulies and ghosties

The only sound in the kitchen of Iron Stone Croft
was the eerie moan of the wind in the roof and
the creaking of old timbers. The fog hung thickly
against the window. For all Holly and her friends
could see, the outside world might have dissolved
away into white nothingness.

The three girls were still seated at the old
oak table.

Holly glanced furtively at her watch. Over half an
hour had gone by since Declan Pallow had issued
his last sinister threat. He was sitting in the chair
by the fireplace, leaning back against the black iron
range. He had picked up the bowl from the floor
and had refilled it with stew from the pot. But the
hand that held the spoon lay limply in his lap.

The three girls looked at one another and Tracy
gave a brief nod. For the last fifteen minutes they
had watched with bated breath as Pallow's head
had slowly fallen forwards, his eyes half-closed.

It was an agonising time. Pallow's head would
dip and his eyes would be on the point of closing

– only for him to rouse himself and stare coldly at them. But each time, his head fell a little further forwards as he succumbed to drowsiness.

Belinda lifted a finger to her lips. Pallow's chin was on his chest, his mouth fallen slack as his breathing deepened. And at last those hooded eyes had closed.

Holly watched him for any sign of movement. But apart from the steady rise and fall of his chest, there was none.

'He's asleep,' Holly mouthed silently.

Belinda and Tracy nodded.

Tracy pointed to each of them then made walking motions with her fingers across the table, followed by a silent hand-mime of overpowering the man.

Belinda shook her head and pointed to the door, looking questioningly at Holly.

Holly looked over at Pallow. It was pretty obvious what her two friends had in mind. Tracy was all for trying to jump him. The more cautious Belinda just wanted to escape.

Pallow's right hand was still in his jacket pocket, although the bulge of the gun was no longer pointed towards them.

If they jumped him, would they have time to get the gun off him? There was a bread knife on the table, but the thought of picking it up and using it to threaten Pallow made Holly's skin crawl.

Holly looked at her friends and tilted her head

towards the door. Tracy and Belinda nodded in agreement.

Very, very slowly Holly slid round in her chair, bringing her legs out from under the table. There was an alarming creak as she lifted her weight from the chair. She paused, half-risen, watching Pallow.

She grimaced as a sharp scrape sounded from the leg of Belinda's chair on the stone floor. All three of them stopped dead, their eyes fixed on the sleeping man. But still he remained undisturbed.

Holly straightened up and crept towards the closed kitchen door. She took hold of the handle and looked round. Belinda and Tracy were both on their feet now.

The grate of metal on metal sounded as Holly turned the handle. There was a hard, dry click as the latch snapped back. Holly gave an inner groan. Even the tiniest sounds seemed magnified out of all proportion. The squelch of Belinda's wet shoes on the stone-flagged floor sounded unbearably loud.

They were all by the door now.

All they needed to do was open the door. A brief dash down the hall. Out through the front door and away! Easy!

Holly drew the door open a fraction.

Cre-e-eak!

They looked at one another in dumb despair. Holly's heart was beating so hard that she was afraid Pallow would hear *that*, never mind the creaking of the old hinges.

Crik! Crik! Cre-eak!

The door was open now – almost enough for them to slide through.

The three girls were as tense as bowstrings. Holly could see into the hallway. The front door was only five metres away.

Belinda looked back at Pallow and her heart jumped into her throat. The hand that held the spoon had slid to one side, the fingers relaxing. And the bowl had tilted and moved, threatening to slide out of his lap.

Pallow stirred in his sleep and the bowl fell with a crash to the floor.

Pallow's eyes opened at the noise. He was alert in an instant. He sprang up, thrusting the hidden gun towards them.

'Get back to the table!' he snarled.

They had failed! Holly's heart sank. They had been so close to escaping!

Pallow rubbed his hands across his eyes as the three girls went forlornly back to the table and sat down.

Pallow stood up and dragged his chair across the floor, kicking the door closed and setting the chair with its back to the entrance. He sat down again.

That's it, Holly thought despairingly. *Even if he nods off again we'll never get past him now.*

'Talk!' said Pallow.

Holly stared at him. 'What do you mean?' she said. 'We've told you everything we know.'

'Just keep talking,' said Pallow. 'I don't care what you talk about.'

Holly realised what he meant. He wanted the noise of their voices to keep him awake.

'I can't think of anything,' said Holly. 'What do you want us to talk about?'

'I don't care,' said Pallow.

Holly's mind was blank.

'What are you planning on doing with us if you get away?' asked Tracy.

'Don't ask stupid questions,' said Pallow.

'I'm only trying to think of something to talk about,' said Tracy. 'You're holding us here at gunpoint, for heaven's sake! What do you expect us to talk about – the weather?'

'I could tell a ghost story,' said Belinda. She looked at Pallow. 'Do you want to hear a ghost story?'

'Go on then,' said Pallow.

'OK,' said Belinda, 'it's a story we were told the other day.' She looked at her friends. 'You know?' she said. 'The one about the werewolf?' She looked at Pallow. 'Apparently, there was a boy who got lost in the hills a long time ago— '

'That's not the werewolf story,' interrupted Tracy. 'You're thinking of the one where the

155

boy gives people drinks out of a leather bottle. That's a different story entirely.'

'No, it isn't,' said Belinda. 'I'm thinking of the story of the boy who turns into a werewolf when the fog comes down. The boy who haunts the hills around here.' She looked at Pallow again. 'I don't suppose you knew this house was haunted, did you? It is, you know. It's the most haunted house in the whole of Scotland.' She took a deep breath. 'He was only fifteen when he disappeared up on the mountains.' She gestured towards the fog-blind window. 'Not far from here. The fog had come down really suddenly, just like it did today. He wandered about lost for hours and hours. Then he found a cave and went to sleep. But it wasn't an ordinary cave. It was full of black magic – and when he woke up he had changed into a werewolf. A huge, ferocious werewolf who leaped on his victims and tore their throats out with huge, bloody fangs.'

As if to give atmosphere to her story, the wind moaned in the rafters – sounding almost human.

Tracy shivered.

Belinda pointed to the window. 'He's out there right now,' she said. 'Creeping through the fog in search of a victim.' Belinda gazed at Declan Pallow. 'Ordinary guns won't stop him,' she said. 'The only thing that will kill him is a silver bullet in the heart. He still lives in the cave, but now the cave is filled with the bones of his victims. And on foggy days like this he comes down the mountains and hammers on the door of this *very* house, looking for victims.'

'Belinda – don't!' said Tracy. She liked ghost stories as much as anyone, but she liked to hear them in the comfort of her own home with her mother close by. Up here in the lonely croft, with the fog all round them and the wind groaning, it was too much. It was too easy to start believing in werewolves.

Belinda sat back. 'That's the legend,' she said. She eyed Pallow. 'I don't suppose you've got any silver bullets in your gun?' she said.

'Funny girl,' Pallow said grimly. 'But I shouldn't worry too much about werewolves if I were you.'

'You never know,' said Belinda. 'I think it's a mistake to dismiss these legends. There's no smoke without fire.'

'I've had enough of this,' said Pallow. He looked at Holly. 'Get a bag,' he said. 'I want you to put all the food you can find in it.'

Holly was just getting up when there was a loud crash from somewhere outside the croft.

Tracy's hands came up to her face, her eyes round with fright. 'What was *that*?' she gasped.

Pallow pulled his chair away from the door and opened it, leaning into the hallway and listening.

'Maybe it's the werewolf,' said Belinda.

'Shut up!' said Pallow. He listened at the door for a while, but there was no further noise.

'I expect it was the wind,' said Holly.

Pallow mumbled something they didn't catch, then turned towards them. 'I told you to pack the food,' he said.

Holly found a cloth bag under the sink and began to fill it.

'You and your stupid stories,' he said, glaring at Belinda as he paced nervously across the kitchen.

'You don't believe in werewolves, do you?' said Belinda.

Pallow waved the hidden gun. 'I believe in this,' he said. He paced to the open door and stared out into the hall. 'How much longer?' they heard him mutter. His patience was wearing thin; they could see that.

Holly crouched by the cupboard under the window, pulling out cans of food and shoving them into the bag. A faint tapping caught her ear, coming from just above her. The furtive sound of fingernails on glass.

She looked up and stifled a scream as she dropped the bag. There was a face at the window – a ghostly, pale face staring in at her. For a split second she thought that Belinda's werewolf story had come true. But it wasn't a werewolf's face that stared anxiously in at her – it was Bobby Talisker!

158

Bobby ducked away as Pallow's head snapped round at the sudden noise from Holly.

Holly stood up, still shaking a little. What was Bobby doing out there?

'Sorry,' she said to Pallow. 'I dropped the bag.' She picked it up and put it on the table. 'I think I've got everything,' she said. 'What do you want me to do now?'

'Nothing,' said Pallow. 'Sit down and shut up.'

'I thought you wanted us to talk,' said Belinda.

Pallow gnawed at his fingernails.

'I want you to shut up!' he snarled. Belinda looked at him. The long wait was really getting to him. She hadn't really expected her ghost story to unnerve him, but she had hoped that it might make him a little more jumpy. He looked like he was on the verge of cracking up anyway.

He didn't sit down again. He paced round the table, the eyes of the three girls following him.

Holly's mind was on Bobby Talisker. The boy must have seen the predicament they were in – but what would he do? Go for help? That would take hours! Anything could happen in that amount of time. Mr Fox could arrive back at the croft at any minute. And once that happened, Pallow would be able to get away – taking them with him. She didn't want to dwell on what might happen after that.

The nervy silence was broken by a loud hammering on the front door. Pallow spun round, his eyes blazing.

Holly jumped up. 'The werewolf!' she screamed, faking panic. 'It's the werewolf!'

'Fool!' spat Pallow, running to the kitchen door and staring out into the hall.

'Now!' yelled Holly, throwing herself towards Pallow. She caught him off guard, cannoning into his back and sending him sprawling into the hallway. As she slammed the kitchen door, she saw him hit against the far wall of the hallway with a shout of rage.

It took Tracy only an instant to react to Holly's sudden charge. She snatched at the chair Pallow had been sitting on earlier and jammed it under the door handle.

'Bobby's out there!' gasped Holly. 'I saw him through the window.'

'Bobby?' exclaimed Belinda. 'How?'

'I don't know,' said Holly.

There was a heavy thud against the kitchen door and the handle rattled. Pallow was trying to get back in.

'Help me!' shouted Tracy, dragging the table towards the door. The three of them sent the heavy old table crashing against the chair that held the door shut. 'We've got to get out of here!'

'The window,' panted Belinda. She jumped and

landed on her knees on top of the cupboard that stood under the window. She thumped her palms up against the sash. The window was paint-encrusted, it looked as though it hadn't been opened in years.

Belinda shook her stinging hands.

'It won't open!' she said desperately.

'Oh, yes it will!' said Tracy. She grabbed the bread knife from the table and sprang up beside Belinda, jamming the blade into the paint-thick gap between the sash and the frame.

'Quick!' yelled Holly, leaning her full weight against the table as blow after blow sounded on the kitchen door. At any moment she dreaded to hear the sound of a bullet being fired through the door.

'Hit it again!' said Tracy as she worked the knife along the side of the window sash. 'I think it's coming!'

Belinda hammered both hands up against the sash. The paint cracked away and the window grated open. Chilling mist boiled in through the gap as Tracy and Belinda forced the sash up.

'Holly!' shouted Tracy. 'Come on!'

Holly sprang towards the window. Belinda was already through it and Tracy had one leg over the sill, pausing for a moment to reach out her hand to Holly.

A wild scraping sounded as Declan Pallow forced

the door open and the legs of the chair and table screeched across the stone floor.

'Stop!' bellowed Pallow, shoving himself in through the narrow gap. 'Stop, or I'll shoot!'

Tracy was through the window now, clinging on to Holly's sleeve to drag her to safety.

Holly gave a final, frantic kick and went tumbling head first through the window.

Tracy hauled her to her feet and almost before she knew what was happening, Holly found herself running through the dense fog.

'This way!' The voice rang uncannily through the fog. Bobby's voice! He appeared ahead of her, catching hold of her arm and pulling her away from the house.

Trees loomed round her as she ran. Tracy was by her side and she could see Belinda only a few paces ahead.

She glanced back and saw the patch of light from the window. And silhouetted against the light she saw the head and shoulders of Declan Pallow.

Freezing air filled her lungs as she ran through the tree-lined blindness of the fog.

There was a yelp and she saw Belinda's dark shape suddenly vanish.

Before Holly had time to wonder what had happened to Belinda, empty air opened out under her feet and she fell with a scream into a terrifying vault of fog.

162

12   Peril on the mountain

Something dark and solid broke out of the fog above Holly's head. She grabbed instinctively at it and found herself swinging in the air, her hands curled round a gnarled old branch. Below her she could hear the crashing of the others as they fell.

Her imagination had time to conjure a precipitous fall below her dangling feet; some dreadful cleft in the hillside down which her friends had plunged. But then she heard a voice.

'Get *off* me, you great lump!' It was Belinda, sounding more annoyed than hurt – and her voice didn't sound very far away.

'Is everyone OK?' That was Bobby's voice, and as Holly looked down, she could see vague shapes only two or three metres beneath her.

'Where's Holly?' Tracy sounded frightened.

'I'm here!' called Holly.

One of the shapes moved up towards her and Bobby's face came out of the fog.

'It's OK,' he said, catching hold of her legs. 'Let go. I'll catch you.'

Holly released her hold and tumbled down into Bobby's waiting arms.

The thick fog had deceived Holly's eyes. It was no cliff that they had run over, but only a steep slope of earth and bracken. Clinging together, the two of them slid down to level ground.

'Are you OK?' asked Bobby.

'Yes, I'm fine,' panted Holly. 'You can let go of me now.'

'Oh – sorry.' Bobby released her.

'I'm out of here,' said Tracy. 'That guy is gonna be on our tails!'

'Which way?' asked Belinda. 'I can't see a thing!'

'Follow me,' said Bobby. 'We've got to get up above the level of the fog if we can.'

'Shush a minute!' said Holly. 'Listen!'

They stood frozen in silence, all ears straining for any sound. The fog was all round them like cotton-wool. They could see one another, and the branches and trunks of nearby trees; but beyond a circle of maybe three metres, everything faded into oblivion.

There was no sound.

'OK,' said Holly, looking at Bobby. 'Let's go.'

Bobby leaned forwards and picked something up. Holly hadn't spotted it before. It was a large black briefcase.

'What have you got there?' asked Holly.

'Pallow's money,' said Bobby. 'I'll explain later. Let's get away from here first.'

Bobby led them up through the trees. The ground was uneven, but it rose steeply all the while.

'Shouldn't we be going downwards?' panted Belinda. 'We want to get back to the loch, don't we?'

'Not yet,' said Bobby. 'We need to get out of this fog first. It's no good us blundering about in all this.'

'How do you know the fog doesn't go right up to the top of the mountains?' asked Tracy.

'It doesn't,' said Bobby. 'Trust me. It'll be lying in the valley. We've only got to climb a little way and we should be above it.'

'You hope!' murmured Belinda.

But Bobby was proved to be right. As they climbed, Holly became aware that she could see a little further all the time until, at last, they came into watery daylight and out of the trees.

The bare mountain side stretched above them, jagged with rocks and crags and patched with heather and gorse. Away above them the upper slopes pushed up into the clouds.

They climbed a little further and came to a halt on a flat outcrop of rock.

Holly looked down into a breathtaking sight. The whole of the countryside below them was drowned in fog. Only a few tall, spiky tree-tops thrust up through the grey gloom. The loch was invisible.

The four of them collapsed on the shoulder of bare rock, panting for breath as they finally had time to rub their aching limbs.

'How did you know we were there?' Holly asked Bobby.

'It's a long story,' said Bobby. He gave Belinda a tired grin. 'Almost as long as your werewolf story.'

'You heard that?' said Belinda. 'How long were you out there?'

'I wasn't outside,' said Bobby. 'I was in the croft. I saw you arrive.'

'What the heck were you doing?' exclaimed Tracy. 'Couldn't you have helped us sooner?'

'I was locked in the garage,' said Bobby. 'You know, the double doors? That's where Gregory Fox keeps his car. He locked me in there.'

Belinda rubbed a weary arm across her eyes. 'Would you like to start making some sense?' she said. 'Why did Mr Fox lock you in his garage, for heaven's sake?'

'And why didn't you go to the police yesterday, like you promised you would?' demanded Tracy.

'OK, OK,' said Bobby, lifting his hands. 'I'll tell you. Don't yell at me.'

'We're not yelling,' said Belinda. 'You'll know quick enough when we start yelling!'

Bobby looked sheepishly at them. 'I wasn't being completely honest with you yesterday,' he began.

'Huh!' Tracy broke in. 'Big surprise!'

'Let him tell us,' said Holly.,

'You know I told you I didn't see who took the case?' Bobby continued. 'Well, that wasn't exactly true. I saw Gregory Fox's car up on the road, before I even knew you were nearby. I crept down through the trees. That's when I saw him coming up the path. I saw he had the bag with him. I knew he must have pulled it up out of the seaweed. At first, I was just going to tell him what it was, but then I thought better of it. If it looked like *he'd* found it, I might not get the reward. So I kept out of sight. He took the bag up to his car and had a look inside. I knew he wouldn't be able to get the case open unless he forced it.'

Bobby thrust his hand in his pocket and produced a small key. 'I'd locked it, you see? And I had the key. I wasn't sure what he'd do. But then he put the bag into the back of his car and drove off.'

Bobby gazed round at the three girls. 'He drove off up the road, towards Iron Stone Croft. The road only leads to the croft in that direction, so I knew he wasn't going straight into town with the case.'

'I guessed it!' said Holly, looking at her friends. 'Didn't I say something like that?' She looked at Bobby. 'And you guessed that if he didn't go straight to Glenroch with the case, he probably wouldn't be taking it down there until the next time he drove in.'

Bobby nodded. 'I know he hates going into town. And he doesn't have a radio, see? So I guessed that he didn't know anything about the missing money; so he wouldn't know what was in the case.'

'Holly worked that out as well,' said Belinda. 'So? What was your plan? To try and sneak the case away from him?' She shook her head. 'I'll say one thing for you – you're persistent. Mad, but persistent!'

'I'm not mad,' said Bobby. 'We need that reward money. If Mr Fox had taken it to the police, we wouldn't have got a penny. And I'd already done so much to try and get it. I couldn't bear the thought of losing it after all that. I had to try and get it back. By the time I'd left you three at the cottage yesterday, it was too late to do anything. So I got up really early this morning and came over here to see if I could get the case back. There was no sign of him when I got to the croft. I got into the garage. The bag was still in the back of the car. He obviously hadn't tried to open the case. He'd just left it there ready to take into town.'

'So you broke into his garage,' said Tracy. 'And then you broke into his car!'

'No!' said Bobby. 'I didn't break in. The garage is kept shut with a bar on the outside. It wasn't locked. And neither was his car. It's a wreck. The back door was held closed with a bit of wire. I didn't have to break into anything. I wouldn't do anything like that.'

'Oh, sure,' said Tracy. 'You're as honest as the day is long!'

'And Mr Fox caught you in there, did he?' asked Holly.

'Very nearly,' said Bobby. 'I'd taken the case out of the bag and I was just about to leave, when I heard him come out of the croft. That ruined everything! I'd intended to take the money out of the case and then put the case back in the car. That way, he could still take the case to the police, and I'd be able to say I found the money somewhere else. But I didn't have time for that. So I shoved a lump of old carpet in the bag and hid behind some rubbish in the back of the garage.' Bobby looked anxiously at the girls, clearly wanting them to realise that he was finally telling them the truth.

'He got into the car and drove it out,' continued Bobby. 'But then he got out again and closed the garage doors before I had a chance to get out. He locked me in there! I tried to get out, but there aren't any windows – and the walls are all solid stone. I tried forcing the doors, but I couldn't get them open. All I could do was sit there and wait for him to come back.' He looked unhappily at them. 'It was really dark in there; the only light came through cracks in the doors. And then it started raining. I thought I'd be locked in there all day.'

'So how did you get out?' asked Belinda.

'I'll explain that in a minute,' said Bobby. 'Anyway the next thing I knew was when I heard your voices. I could see you through the cracks in the doors. I was going to shout for help – until I saw that man with you. I realised it had to be Declan Pallow when I saw the cut on his head. I didn't know what to do. I could see you were in trouble. But then this light appeared up near the roof of the garage. There's a sort of ventilation hole – a missing stone. So I climbed up on some rubbish, and I could hear you talking.' He looked at Belinda. 'You think I'm mad? From what I heard, that Pallow is the mad one. He had a gun, didn't he?'

'That's right,' said Tracy. 'If he hadn't, we'd have had him hog-tied in ten seconds flat. He could hardly stand up.'

'Yes, I guessed he must be in a pretty bad way,' said Bobby. 'I heard Belinda tell her story – and I heard that bit about the werewolf hammering on the door. I thought if I could just get out, I could bash on the door and you'd be able to jump him while he was wondering what was out there. And now that there was a bit of light in there, I was able to find a crowbar to force the garage doors.'

'The crash!' said Holly. 'We thought it was the wind knocking something over. It was you!'

170

'That's right,' said Bobby. 'I knew you'd hear it, but I hoped no one would come to investigate.' He grinned. 'Especially not after Belinda's ghost story. Then I went round to the window to check you were OK.'

'And nearly frightened the life out of me,' said Holly. 'I thought you *were* the werewolf!'

'Yes, sorry about that,' said Bobby, still grinning. 'but I had to try and let you know I was there, so you'd know what to do when I knocked on the door. But how on earth did you get caught by Pallow?'

Now it was time for the girls to explain. They told him about the strange man on the motorboat, and how they had assumed it must be Declan Pallow – until they had encountered Pallow himself on Innis Maer.

Bobby put his hands over his face. 'The car,' he said. 'Was it a battered old orange estate car?'

'Yes,' said Holly, puzzled. 'Do you know it?'

'Of course I know it,' said Bobby. 'That's Gregory Fox's car!'

'Oh, crumbs,' said Belinda. 'So the man we jumped on must have been Mr Fox! Holly, you *idiot!*'

'How was I supposed to know?' said Holly.

It really wasn't her fault. How could she have known that the man she had seen acting suspiciously in the woods a few days back was only

171

the strange old recluse from Iron Stone Croft? And when she saw the man again – in that same blue anorak – of course she assumed it was Declan Pallow. What else was she supposed to think?

'I thought he'd broken into the cottage,' she said. 'I thought he'd stolen the key to the boat and was trying to make a getaway.' She looked at Tracy. '*You* thought so, too.'

'Yeah,' said Tracy. 'But only because you were so convinced. That poor old man! He must have thought the sky had fallen in on him!'

'But what was he doing in the cottage?' said Holly. 'And how did he get the boat key?'

'We can worry about that later,' said Belinda.

'He wasn't hurt, was he?' asked Bobby.

'He was pretty wet by the time we'd finished with him,' said Belinda. 'But I don't think we did him any real damage. Crumbs! Talk about looking before you leap!' She looked at Holly. 'I am never, ever, *ever* going to listen to you again!'

'Oh, that's right,' said Holly. 'Blame me!'

'Who else is there to blame?' demanded Belinda. 'This whole thing is your fault.'

'But I was right,' said Holly. 'I said all along that Pallow was hiding round here. And he was! And we've got the money now. All we've got to do is take it to the police. We can tell them the whole thing.'

'The *whole* thing?' said Bobby unhappily.

'Yes!' insisted Belinda. 'The whole story. And this time we're going to the police with you.'

Bobby stared miserably at the ground. 'We won't get the reward now, will we? After everything we've been through.'

'You can bank on that,' said Tracy. 'The police are going to come down on you like a ton of bricks.'

'Oh, yes,' said Belinda. 'Speaking of which, I think you're going to find your boss at the hotel isn't too pleased with you right now, either.'

Bobby gave the briefcase a kick. 'I should have left it in the plane!' he said. 'I wish I'd never even seen it!'

'We'll tell the police why you took it,' said Holly, trying to sound comforting.

'Yes,' said Belinda. 'And that's going to be *some* journey in this weather.'

The wind had risen again, blowing their hair around their faces and creeping in under their clothes. Above them the clouds were moving heavily across the mountains and below them they could see wisps and curls of mist being torn from the dense grey mass of fog.

'This is all we need,' said Belinda, wrapping her jacket round herself. 'If we don't get lost forever in that fog, we'll be blown off the mountain and never heard of again!'

They all stood up, shivering with the cold.

'If we head that way,' said Bobby, pointing

northwards, 'we'll come to a track that will take us down the hillside to the end of the loch. It should be easy enough to find. There's only one problem.'

'And what's that?' asked Tracy.

'There's some pretty rough land between us and the track,' said Bobby. He looked at them. 'I hope you're not scared of heights.'

Holly and Tracy looked at Belinda. Belinda was known to get dizzy spells from looking out of an upstairs window.

Belinda gave a heavy sigh.

'Can't we just go down the hillside from here?' she said. 'We'd end up at the loch just the same.'

'I wouldn't want to risk it,' said Bobby. 'Pallow is down in that fog somewhere. The last thing we want is to bump into him again. We've got to put as much distance as we can between us and him – at least until we get somewhere where we can see a wee bit better.' He gave Belinda a reassuring smile. 'Don't worry,' he said. 'I'll hold your hand all the way.'

'Oh, no you *won't*!' said Belinda. 'I can hold my own hand, thank you very much. Come on, let's get it over with, if we have to. But just do me one favour, will you?'

'What?' asked Bobby.

'Just don't tell me how dangerous it is, OK?' said

Belinda. 'I don't want to know. I really don't want to know!'

Holly stood at the sharp edge of rock and looked down into the deep gorge that lay across their path.

It was the first major obstacle they'd come to. Up until then it had been a case of scrambling over and round boulders and rocks. They'd done their best to keep walking as stones went tumbling down the mountainside from beneath their feet.

At first, things had seemed to be going well. The wind was a constant problem, but at least it seemed to be clearing the sky of the thicker clouds. The glimpse of blue sky that Holly had seen all that time ago on the island was spreading as the clouds thinned. And there was some sign that the fog was being swept away, too, as more treetops began to emerge out of the grey gloom.

Holly had even felt heartened enough to give a hopeful cheer as the watery disc of the sun had appeared through the clouds.

And then they had come to the gorge; a deep cleft clawed out of the mountainside across their path. They had stared across at the far lip of rock, nearly two metres away at its narrowest point. Their ears were filled with a rush of water that cascaded deep down in the cloven heart of the gorge.

'If we take a good run up,' Bobby told them, 'we'll get across easily.'

He stepped right up to the edge, swinging the case in both hands and then launching it into the air with a shout. The case crashed to ground about half a metre beyond the far lip of rock. Now all they had to do was follow it!

Bobby went first, pacing back the way they had come and then turning to face the cleft. He took a couple of deep breaths before gathering himself and running for the edge.

Holly's heart missed a beat as Bobby seemed to hang for a split second over the dark chasm. But he landed safely on the far side without even losing his footing.

'It's just like I said,' he called back with a grin. 'It's easy!'

'Who's next?' asked Tracy. 'Belinda?'

'Uh – no. You two go first,' said Belinda.

Holly walked back to the place from which Bobby had started his run. From this angle the mouth of the ragged gorge looked deceptively narrow.

She took a deep, steadying breath, bounced on her heels a couple of times and then ran.

Her foot came thudding down on the very lip of the cleft. For a heart-stopping moment the throat of the gorge opened up under her before she came to a jarring landing well over the far side. She

176

stumbled with the force of her leap and Bobby caught her arm.

'Well done!' he said.

Holly heard a yell behind her.

'*Geronimo!*' shrieked Tracy as she came sailing across the gap, her arms stretched out for balance as she landed sure-footedly as a mountain goat.

The three of them looked back to where Belinda stood.

She gave them a sickly grin.

'I don't think I can do it,' she said.

'Sure you can,' said Tracy.

Belinda edged close to the lip of rock.

'Don't look down!' yelled Holly.

But it was too late. Belinda stared down into the gulf for only a moment. Her head reeled as the entire chasm seemed to swim in front of her eyes.

'I'm sorry,' she said, backing away. 'I can't do it. I just can't do it!'

13 An unwelcome guest

Belinda stared across the gaping chasm. Holly, Tracy and Bobby had gathered at the far lip of rock, their faces concerned as they looked back at her.

She shook her head. 'I can't do it,' she said again.

'It's not even two metres,' said Holly. 'You can jump that easily.'

'Isn't there some other way down?' said Belinda.

'There is,' said Bobby. 'But I wouldn't recommend it.' He pointed down the mountainside. 'The rockface is really unstable down there,' he said. 'You could easily end up setting off a rock fall.'

'You see?' said Tracy. 'You haven't got any choice!'

'OK!' shouted Belinda, her fear making her angry. 'OK, I'll do it. Just give me a minute or two.'

'Don't think about it,' said Bobby. 'You'll only make it worse.'

'Worse?' Belinda muttered as she shuffled backwards away from the chasm. 'How could I possibly make it *worse*?'

'Think brave thoughts,' shouted Tracy.

Belinda scuffed her shoes in the muddy ground and gave Tracy an irritated glare. But it wasn't Tracy who was the source of Belinda's irritation. Belinda was annoyed with herself.

She *could* jump two metres. At least, if someone were to draw lines on the ground two metres apart, she could launch herself from one and land easily beyond the other. So why couldn't she do it now? What was the difference?

Belinda smiled grimly to herself. *The difference is that I've got this little voice in my head, telling me I'm going to get killed if I fall! That's the difference!*

She rubbed her hands together, trying to ignore the fluttering in her stomach.

She ran. The dark crack came wavering towards her, growing wider and wider.

At the last possible moment she skidded to a halt with a scream of frustration.

'I *can't!*' she shouted.

'OK,' said Tracy. 'It's OK.' She looked at Holly. 'I'll go back over and help her,' she said.

Belinda felt even worse about herself as she saw the easy way that Tracy ran and jumped the cleft.

'I don't know what's wrong with me,' said Belinda.

'It's fear of heights,' said Tracy. 'You can't help it. Now, take hold of my hand. We'll do it together.'

Belinda took Tracy's hand and the two of them backed away from the chasm.

'I'll count down from three,' said Tracy. 'And then we run for it.'

'You won't let go, will you?' said Belinda.

'Nope,' said Tracy, giving Belinda's hand a reassuring squeeze. 'Ready?'

'Not really.'

Tracy frowned at her.

Belinda nodded miserably. 'Ready,' she said.

'Three . . . two . . . one . . . GO!' yelled Tracy.

Belinda hardly knew what was going on. She could feel Tracy's hand tight in hers, and she could feel the jarring of her feet on the ground as they ran forwards.

'Jump!' yelled Tracy.

Belinda closed her eyes and leaped. The next thing she knew was when her feet came crashing down safely on the far side.

Holly and Bobby grabbed her as she stumbled forwards, laughing with relief.

'Easy!' Belinda gasped as she staggered to a stop. She grinned round at them. 'I don't know what you were making such a fuss about,' she said. 'That was a piece of cake!'

'What *we* were making a fuss about?' said Tracy with a laugh. 'I like that!'

'Are you feeling a bit more confident now?' Bobby asked Belinda.

'A *lot* more confident,' said Belinda.

'That's good,' said Bobby. 'Because the next crack is twice that wide.'

'What?' Belinda gaped at him. But then she saw the grin on his face.

'I'm only kidding you,' said Bobby. 'Actually, it's all pretty straightforward from here on. We've done the most difficult bit.'

'Have we?' said Belinda. 'My feet are freezing. And my fingers are freezing. And my ears are freezing. And my *nose* is freezing!' She looked at Bobby. 'I'm freezing in places I didn't even know I had. How far to this path you were telling us about?'

'Not far, now,' said Bobby, picking up the case.

'Are there really any more obstacles like that?' asked Holly, glancing back into the mouth of the gorge.

'No. It's a lot easier from here on,' said Bobby.

They trekked silently across the mountain, too tired and cold to speak. But Bobby was right. Despite the odd shoulder of rock that needed climbing or circling, the way forwards was a lot easier than it had been before they had encountered the gorge.

At least, it *was* easier, until they came to a place strewn with stones. It was steep, and the stones were constantly rolling away from under their feet as they picked their way through them.

182

'Careful,' warned Belinda, as Tracy moved surefootedly ahead of them.

'It's easy,' said Tracy, looking over her shoulder. 'We want to get out of here as quickly as possible, don't we?'

'You'll fall over,' said Belinda.

'Nonsense!' said Tracy. She was very proud of her fitness. The last thing she was going to do was fall over.

She gave a yell as a stone shifted unexpectedly under her foot. Her arms waved as she slid, losing balance and landing on her backside in a sudden rush of loosened stones.

She slid a couple of metres in a flurry of tumbling stones before she managed to scrabble to a halt. Rocks and stones went bouncing down the mountainside.

She glared round at Belinda. 'That was your fault!' she said.

'What did *I* do?' asked Belinda. 'I wasn't anywhere near you.'

Tracy got cautiously to her feet and climbed back up to the others.

'You said I was going to fall,' she said. 'You put a jinx on me.'

'Are you OK?' asked Bobby.

'Of course I'm OK,' said Tracy, her hands on her hips as she frowned at Belinda. 'If you hadn't told me to be careful, I wouldn't have looked round.

183

And if I hadn't looked round, I wouldn't have fallen.'

Holly laughed. 'It sounds like you've got a bad case of hurt pride there, Tracy,' she said. 'You know what they say – pride goes before a fall.'

Belinda was grinning.

'I don't know what's so funny,' said Tracy. 'And after all I did to help you over that crack. I should have left you there!'

'Shall we get on?' said Bobby.

'Yes,' said Belinda, still grinning. 'Do you want me to hold your hand, Tracy?'

'Oh, nuts!' said Tracy. 'Let's get out of here!'

The sky was brightening all the time, and suddenly the sun broke free of the clouds and a delightful warmth beat on their faces as the steep mountainside was bathed in sunlight.

'There!' cried Bobby. 'There's the path!'

It was obviously well-used; a narrow, snaking path made by the passage of countless feet. Stones lined the way as it zigzagged up the mountain's flank.

'The fog's clearing,' said Holly. Where all had been lost in the grey blanket, pieces of landscape now jutted out into clear air, although the loch itself was still hidden.

They reached the path and began the long scramble down.

It was depressing to have to sink once again

into the mist as they descended. The sun lost all its power to warm them – becoming once again a pale, wintry disc as they lost sight of mountains, trees and everything.

'What do you think Pallow has been up to all this time?' asked Tracy. 'I guess he hasn't just been sitting there twiddling his thumbs.'

'Do you think he'd have followed us?' asked Belinda.

'I don't think he can have done,' said Bobby. 'We'd have seen him. And anyway, from what you said, he'd never be able to get across that gorge. Not in the state he was in.'

Holly nodded thoughtfully. 'Either he's stayed in the croft in the hope that Mr Fox would arrive and he'd be able to use the car to escape, or he's made a run for it.'

'He must know we'd go straight to the police,' said Belinda.

'Yes,' said Holly, 'but he'd know it would take us some time before we could raise the alarm. He might be hoping Mr Fox would turn up in time for him to get away.'

'Or he might have decided to try it on foot,' said Tracy. 'All this fog would keep him well hidden. It would be just our luck to crash right into him.'

'Don't even *think* about that,' said Belinda. 'Not after all we've been through to get away from him.'

185

'I don't think that will happen,' said Bobby. 'If he left the croft, he'd have used the road. We've come the long way round. He'd be well ahead of us.'

'Well, he'd better not escape,' said Belinda. 'Not after what we had to put up with from him back there.'

The steep side of the mountain began to level out. The mist was thinning all the time, and now they could see for fifty metres or so. They came to a vivid green marshy area of hummocky heather and smooth, grassy creases.

'We're almost there,' said Bobby. 'The road is just beyond those trees.'

They followed the mountain path into the trees and came down on to the long curve of the road that wound round the loch. It was their first sight of the long, still waters of Loch Evayne for some time. The water was as dull as lead, but at last they knew they were on the final leg to the cottage.

'We could make better time if we jogged,' said Tracy. 'And it'd warm us up.'

'I can't *jog*!' said Belinda. 'I can hardly walk!'

'Think of a hot shower,' said Tracy, linking her arm through Belinda's. 'Think of dry clothes and hot food.'

'And think of Declan Pallow behind bars,' said Holly, linking up with Belinda's other arm. She hooked an arm for Bobby and the four of them began to walk briskly abreast along the road.

'This is like a scene from the *Wizard of Oz*!' said Belinda. 'When they all go prancing down the yellow brick road.'

'That's right!' laughed Tracy. 'I'll be Dorothy!' She began to sing. 'We're off to see the Wizard, the wonderful Wizard of Oz!'

No one who saw them, as they marched singing along the road, would have thought that they had just made a perilous escape from a half-crazed gunman.

But it wasn't long before the cold and the exhaustion of their flight took its toll, and by the time they came to familiar ground they were walking slowly on numbed feet and longing for their ordeal to be over.

Mr Fox's abandoned car loomed out of the mist, its door still open.

'He didn't come back for it,' said Holly. 'I wonder why? He was soaked; you'd think he'd have gone straight back to the croft.'

'It's a good thing he didn't,' said Tracy. 'Or who knows where we'd be by now.'

'Yes, but why *didn't* he?' puzzled Holly. 'Where else could he have gone?'

Holly's question remained unanswered as Bay View Cottage appeared at last through the mist.

'We'll phone the police before we do anything

else,' said Holly as they climbed over the low wall. Christina's car was still missing, and the front door was still ajar.

Holly ran to the telephone and tapped out 999. The others gathered round her as she held the receiver to her ear. Her hands were so cold that it was all she could do to keep her fingers closed round the receiver.

She gave a grimace of annoyance and jabbed her finger down on the release button on the cradle.

'What's up?' asked Belinda.

'I don't know,' said Holly. 'I can't hear anything.' She stabbed at the button a few times, but the telephone remained obstinately silent. She held the receiver out to the others.

'The line's dead,' she said dully.

'Give it here,' said Belinda. 'You're probably doing it all wrong.' She took the receiver and prodded at the button on the top of the telephone.

'It's no good,' she said. 'I think the line must be dead.'

'I just told you that!' said Holly. 'Is it plugged in properly?'

Tracy leaned over the sofa, following the cable to the wall socket. 'Everything looks OK back here,' she said. 'There must be something wrong further down the line.'

'Great!' groaned Belinda. 'Now what do we do?'

'There are phones at the hotel,' said Bobby. 'Maybe they'll be working.'

'Yes,' said Belinda. 'And maybe they won't. Maybe the rain has got into the works and blown the lot!'

'We'll have to go to the hotel,' said Holly. 'We've got to tell *someone* what's been going on. And even if the phones aren't working, someone will be able to drive us into town for the police.'

'Wait a sec,' said Belinda as she jammed the receiver back on to the useless cradle. 'I'm going to put some dry clothes on first.'

'Belinda!' shouted Tracy as her friend bounded up the stairs. 'We don't have *time* for this!'

'Two seconds!' Belinda called back.

'Pallow is going to get away,' said Tracy, looking at Bobby and Holly.

'But at least he hasn't got the money,' said Holly. 'And at least we didn't end up getting shot!'

Tracy went to the sitting-room door. 'Belinda!' she yelled up the stairs. 'Get a move on!' There was no sound from Belinda. 'Heck!' said Tracy. 'We could all have changed in the time she's taking. Belinda!'

'Don't yell at her,' said Bobby. 'She did really well back there – for someone who's scared of heights.'

Tracy stared at him. 'I'll yell at her if I want,' she said. 'She's *my* friend. Anyway, she expects it.' She

189

made an impatient sound through her nose. 'I'm going to go and drag her down here,' she said.

She raced up the stairs and round into the upper hallway.

'Belinda, if you don't— ' Her voice stopped abruptly.

Holly and Bobby looked at each other.

There was absolute silence from upstairs.

Something was wrong up there. Holly could *feel* it. She went to the foot of the stairs.

'Tracy?' she called. 'Are you OK?'

Bobby stood next to her, both of them looking anxiously up the stairwell.

Tracy appeared at the head of the stairs.

'I think we're in trouble,' she said.

'What's happened?' asked Holly, her heart fluttering as she looked up at Tracy's ashen face. 'Is Belinda OK?'

Tracy's face twisted. 'Not really,' she said, her eyes flickering sideways.

There was a flurry of movement at the head of the stairs and Tracy gave a gasp as Declan Pallow stepped out from the shadows of the wall. His hand snaked round her neck, the other hand clenched in the pocket of his jacket, the hidden point of his gun jabbing into Tracy's ribs.

'Stay right where you are!' snarled Pallow. 'This time you *won't* get away!'

14 A switch

Holly hesitated for a moment. The open front door of the cottage was only a metre behind her. If she moved quickly, maybe she could fling herself through the door before Pallow had the chance to react. She could run for help!

Her brain whirled. Run? All the way to the hotel? And what would Pallow be doing with her friends in the meantime?

Pallow jerked the hidden gun into Tracy's side again.

'Where's the case?' he snarled.

At least now Holly understood why the telephone wasn't working. Pallow must have disabled it.

Holly was about to speak when a sudden sound made her pause. It was the bark of a dog somewhere outside the cottage. Rosie! It had to be Rosie!

Holly hadn't given any thought to Christina's dog. The last time any of them had mentioned her had been when Tracy had said she hoped Rosie had found somewhere dry to shelter from the rain.

The barking became continuous and grew louder. Rosie had obviously come back from some hiding-place and had picked up the scent of danger – the smell of a stranger in the cottage. An interloper who needed to be seen off.

Holly glanced over her shoulder and saw Rosie through the glass panel of the door, galloping towards the cottage over the grass.

'Get that door shut!' shouted Pallow. 'Don't let that thing in here!'

'Don't hurt her!' cried Holly as Rosie hurled herself against the half-open door in a wild frenzy of barking.

'Keep it away!' Pallow almost screamed.

As Rosie pounced up the stairs, Holly managed to grab her collar. By the panic in Pallow's face, it was obvious that he was terrified of the dog. Holly was frightened that he might simply shoot Rosie.

Rosie twisted and turned in Holly's grip, snarling and scrabbling at the stairs as she tried to get free.

'Don't shoot her!' shouted Holly, pulling back on the dog's collar with all her strength. She managed to drag Rosie away from the stairs and push her in through the sitting-room door. She released the collar and slammed the door. Frantic barking and the noise of claws on wood sounded from beyond the door as Rosie tried to get out.

Holly gasped for breath as she stared up the stairs at Pallow's ashen face. A suspicion began to grow in her mind. It was something that she hadn't thought about in all the time they had been held captive. But it came creeping into her mind now, as she looked at Pallow.

Why had he never shown his gun?

'Is that door shut properly?' said Pallow, his pale face running with sweat.

'Yes,' said Holly.

Pallow glanced along the upper hallway. 'You!' he said to Belinda. 'Get down there.'

Belinda sidled past him and walked down to join Bobby and Holly. Pallow followed her, still keeping a tight grip round Tracy's neck.

'That car out there,' he said, jerking his head to indicate Gregory Fox's abandoned car. 'What's it doing there?'

'It isn't doing anything,' said Belinda.

'Don't get smart with me, girl,' snarled Pallow. 'Why is it there with the door open? Whose car is it?'

'It belongs to the man who owns the croft you were keeping us in,' said Holly. 'He's round here somewhere. And when he sees you he'll go straight to the police.'

'Then I'd better not waste any more time,' said Pallow. He stared at Bobby. 'Where's the case?'

Bobby glanced over his shoulder at the door of the sitting-room. Wild barking and scrabbling still sounded from the room beyond.

193

'In there,' said Bobby. 'Why don't you go and get it?'

'I don't think so,' said Pallow. '*You* get it. And I'm warning you – if you let that animal out, I'll shoot it in its tracks.'

Bobby hesitated.

'Do it, Bobby,' gasped Tracy, Pallow's arm still across her throat. 'Just give him the money.'

Bobby nodded. He edged the sitting-room door open. Holly saw a glimpse of Rosie's muzzle as Bobby slid round into the room and closed the door again.

'Good girl, good girl,' came Bobby's muffled voice. 'Calm down. There's a good girl. It's OK. Everything's OK.'

Holly looked at Pallow. 'You won't be able to get away in the car,' she said. 'There aren't any keys.'

'I know how to start a car without keys,' said Pallow.

Suddenly Tracy let out a gasp and began to breathe with difficulty, gasping in air through her open mouth and clutching at Pallow's arm with her hands.

'You're hurting her!' shouted Belinda. 'Let her go!'

Tracy had been waiting for a chance to try something like this. Something to distract Pallow long enough for the three of them to turn the tables on him.

'I can't breathe!' she gurgled, her breath rasping in her throat. 'You're choking me!'

'Let her go!' shouted Holly, guessing immediately what Tracy was up to.

Tracy allowed herself to become a dead weight against Pallow, pulling him down as her legs collapsed and she sank to the floor.

Belinda and Holly ran forwards. Pallow's hand came out of his pocket and hit against the wall to save himself from falling over.

As Holly bumped up against Pallow, the back of her hand struck against the side of his jacket. There was something solid in his pocket – but it didn't feel large or heavy enough to be a gun. And it was the wrong shape, too.

An instant later Pallow released his arm from round Tracy's neck and sprang backwards, his hand knifing back into his pocket.

'No tricks!' he shouted.

'You nearly strangled her!' Belinda said, kneeling over Tracy as she lay curled up, gasping for breath on the floor.

At that moment Bobby came edging out of the sitting-room with the case.

'Don't give it to him!' shouted Holly. 'He hasn't got a gun! I felt it! It isn't a gun!'

Tracy and Belinda stared at Holly, but before they had the chance to say or do anything, Pallow sprang forward, wrenching the case out of Bobby's hands.

'Get back!' Pallow shouted, swinging the case so that Bobby was forced to back away across the small lobby.

'Don't let him go!' shouted Tracy. 'Grab him!'

Belinda and Tracy scrambled to their feet. Pallow came slowly towards them, swinging the case menacingly in his hands.

'Very clever,' he snarled at Holly. 'But a wee bit too late, I think.' He lunged with the case and the four youngsters fell back. Pallow was by the open front door now.

He swung the case at them a final time, then darted out through the door and ran across the wet grass towards Gregory Fox's abandoned car.

'Don't let him get away!' shouted Tracy.

'It doesn't matter,' said Bobby. 'Let him go. It doesn't matter!'

'But he's got the money!' said Belinda.

'That's what *he* thinks,' said Bobby. He pulled open the sitting-room door. Rosie came pelting out, jumping up at them and barking madly.

'That way!' said Holly. 'Rosie! That way! Go get him!'

Rosie hurtled out through the front door and went streaking across the grass. Holly and the others piled out of the cottage. Pallow was almost at the car by then. His head snapped round as he heard the dog coming after him. He stumbled, swinging the case to try and ward Rosie off, as he tumbled head first into the car and yanked the door shut.

Rosie jumped up at the car window, barking and snarling. Holly could see Pallow's face through the windscreen for a moment, then it ducked down.

'What's he doing?' said Belinda. 'He hasn't got the key.'

'He's going to try and hot-wire it, I bet!' said Tracy. 'Oh, heck! He's going to get away.'

'Will you listen to me!' yelled Bobby. 'Let him go!' He grabbed Holly by the arm and towed her into the cottage.

'Bobby! What on earth are you doing!' Holly said as he dragged her into the sitting-room.

'Look!' said Bobby. Holly followed the line of his pointing finger.

'Oh!' Bundles of bank-notes were heaped on the couch.

'I've had the key to the case all along,' said Bobby. 'It only took me a couple of seconds to tip out the money and shove in a load of old papers I found in here. You see? Even if he gets away, he hasn't got the money!'

Tracy came running into the sitting-room.

'He can't get the car going,' she said breathlessly. She stared at the heap of bundled bank-notes. 'What on earth!'

Holly was laughing. 'Bobby took the money out of the case.'

There was a shrill whistle from outside.

'Belinda!' said Tracy. The three of them ran out to find that Belinda had run down to the wall and was standing on it, yelling and waving her arms.

It only took them a moment to see what she was waving and yelling at. A car was coming up the road from the direction of the hotel.

'That's Mr Williamson's car,' said Bobby. He jumped over the wall as the car slewed to a halt.

The car doors were flung open and the driver and passengers got out. Holly recognised the driver as the man from the hotel. The two passengers were Christina McKetchnie and Gregory Fox.

'It's Pallow!' shouted Bobby. 'We've got Pallow!'

'What are you talking about, lad?' said Mr Williamson.

Bobby pointed over to the other car. Rosie was still at the driver's door, crouched and snarling as Pallow stared out at her. He seemed to have given up hope of getting the car started and was sitting there staring at the growling dog with hollow, hooded eyes.

'My car!' exclaimed Mr Fox. 'And these are the young hooligans who attacked me!'

'We're not hooligans,' said Belinda, almost laughing. 'We thought you were someone else. We thought you were Declan Pallow!'

Christina stared over at Gregory Fox's car. 'Good heavens!' she gasped. 'It *is* Pallow!'

'He pretended he had a gun,' said Holly. 'He held us captive. But it isn't really a gun at all.'

Mr Williamson sprinted over to the car.

'OK, Rosie,' he said, taking the dog by the collar. 'Good girl!' He pulled the car door open and leaned into the car. 'I hear you've been frightening the wee lassies, Mr Pallow. Would you care to try your nasty tricks out on me?'

Pallow's head fell forwards on to the steering-wheel. There was no fight left in him.

Mr Williamson straightened up. 'I don't think we'll be having any trouble from Mr Pallow,' he called. 'Would one of you care to call the police on my car phone?'

One of the police cars had already gone, taking Declan Pallow away with it.

The policeman had taken a broken metal rod out of Pallow's jacket pocket. All the while the girls had thought they were being menaced by a gun, all Pallow had in his pocket was that piece of broken metal!

Pallow's expression had been priceless when he had been told that the case he had worked so hard to recover didn't have anything other than holiday brochures in it.

And once Pallow had been dealt with, Bobby and the girls told the remaining policeman everything that had happened.

The policeman's face became grave as Bobby confessed to having hidden the money.

'He only did it so the reward could be used to buy land for the bird sanctuary,' said Belinda.

'Aye,' said the policeman, frowning at Bobby. 'That's as may be. But it's no excuse for what you did, lad. I shall have to report this to my superiors.'

'Oh, Bobby,' said Christina. 'You must have known you were doing wrong!'

'But it all came out OK in the end, didn't it?' said Holly. 'I mean, Bobby helped us capture Pallow and get the money back, didn't he?'

The policeman nodded and folded up his notepad. 'I'm sure everything will be taken into account at the appropriate time,' he said.

'Could you just tell me one thing?' said Bobby. '*Was* there a reward for finding the money?'

The policeman shrugged. 'I couldn't tell you. But I don't think *you'll* be seeing any of it, if there is. Not after your antics these past few days!'

It didn't take long for the rest of the picture to fall into place for the girls.

The most puzzling thing for Holly was what Gregory Fox had been up to.

It turned out that Mr Fox had a key to Bay View Cottage, given to him some time ago by Christina so that he could use their phone in an emergency if she and her husband were out. That was how

Mr Fox got into the cottage in the first place. And the reason why he wanted to get into the cottage was because his car had broken down in the road. Initially he had intended phoning for a mechanic, but finding the phone engaged, he had decided to take Christina's boat down the loch to Glenroch and speak to the mechanic in person.

That was when the girls had spotted him.

Once he had recovered from being hurled into the water, he had made his way to the Angel Hotel, where they had given him dry clothes and put him in front of a warm fire while they phoned round to try and find Christina.

It had taken most of the afternoon to track Christina down, but once she heard that Mr Fox had been thrown off her boat by three wild girls, she went straight to the hotel.

Mr Williamson had agreed to come up to the cottage with Christina and Mr Fox to see exactly what was going on.

Which was when they found Pallow trapped by Rosie in the immobile car, and Holly and the others all talking at once about a fake gun and an adventure on the mountain and a briefcase that *wasn't* full of money!

The day didn't quite end with the departure of Bobby and the last policeman. In the early evening the girls heard a motorboat chugging across the loch, towing Christina's boat back to the jetty.

'And now,' said Christina, once the three girls had helped her tie the retrieved boat up, 'I think we could all do with a good night's sleep.' She shook her head. 'Heaven only knows how I'm going to explain this to your parents.'

Holly laughed. 'I shouldn't worry too much,' she said. 'They're getting used to our adventures.'

'Yeah,' sighed Belinda as they trudged back through the chill of evening to the cottage. '*They* might be, but *I'm* not!'

The following morning brought the policeman back to Bay View Cottage with some very good news for the three girls.

They were in the middle of breakfast and Christina poured him a cup of tea as he sat at the table with them.

'You'll no doubt be pleased to hear that the Talisker lad is in no trouble,' said the policeman. 'We've decided to overlook his behaviour in the circumstances. Although he's been told to use his brains a wee bit more from now on.'

'And was there a reward?' asked Holly. 'For finding the money, I mean?'

'Aye,' said the policeman. 'There's a five thousand pounds reward.'

'Wow,' breathed Tracy. 'So Bobby will get the money for the bird sanctuary after all!'

'Now, that brings me to the other thing I was asked to come here and tell you,' said the policeman with a smile. 'The reward will not be going to young master Talisker.' He leaned across the table, his eyebrows raised. 'The reward is going to you three lassies!'

They stared speechlessly at him as he poured a spoonful of sugar into his tea and slowly stirred it.

'Five thousand pounds?' gasped Holly. 'For us?'

'Aye,' said the policeman. 'That's what I've been told.' He took a sip of tea. 'You're to receive a cheque from the insurance firm for five thousand pounds.'

Holly swallowed hard. She'd had some shocks in her time, but this was unbelievable!

'Christina?' asked Belinda. 'Do you know how much it will cost to buy the land for the bird sanctuary?'

'Over seven thousand pounds, I'm afraid,' said Christina.

Belinda looked at her two friends.

'Well?' she said. 'What do you say?'

Holly grinned. 'Of course!' She felt a real sense of relief. She could have coped with a reward of ten pounds, or even a hundred pounds – but the thought of five thousand pounds made her head spin. 'Tracy? What do you think?'

'I think it's a brilliant idea!' said Tracy. She looked

at the policeman. 'Can we just hand the money over to help towards buying the land for the bird sanctuary?'

'It'll be your money,' said the policeman. 'I dare say you can do what you like with it.'

'I really think you should take some time to think this through,' said Christina. 'That's an awful lot of money. Think of all the things you could do with it.'

'I'm thinking of that right now,' said Holly, looking at her two friends. They nodded at her and she smiled at Christina. 'We're going to donate the money to the bird sanctuary fund!' She laughed. 'On one condition, though.'

'What's that?' asked Christina.

'That we can be there to see Bobby's face when he finds out!' said Holly. 'I wouldn't miss seeing that for *ten* thousand pounds!'